BRETHREN

BRETHREN

Leonard Leventon

Northwest Publishing Inc.
Salt Lake City, Utah

Brethren

This is a work of fiction.
All characters and events portrayed in this book are fictional,
and any resemblance to real people is purely coincidental.
For information address: Northwest Publishing Inc.,
6906 South 300 West, Salt Lake City, Utah 84047

BCC 04.20.94

PRINTING HISTORY
First Printing 1994

ISBN 1-56901-400-0

NPI books are published by Northwest Publishing Incorporated,
6906 South 300 West, Salt Lake City, Utah 84047.
The name "NPI" and the "NPI" logo are trademarks belonging to
Northwest Publishing Incorporated.

PRINTED IN TNE UNITED STATES OF AMERICA
10 9 8 7 6 5 4 3 2 1

Dedicated to my wife Edit,
without whom this book would be
meaningless.

ONE

A knot of cold hard fear settled into my stomach. It happened to be there before. I can't remember the first time I felt it. At least, I tell myself that from time to time.

This time it had nothing to do with—what *was* her name?—This time was not my first date with Judy in the eighth grade. But it was a date with some kind of destiny for me. Why had I answered that ad in the newspaper? Why did I really agree to carry this package clear across the Atlantic to the south of France for free airfare? I could easily have afforded the plane ticket. First class.

The street in Antibes was perfect. Small European houses lined the block, but not quite in symmetry. There was a natural carefreeness to the order.

What was waiting for me in number cinq Rue Mouette? I was about to find out.

I walked up gently as I could to the front door and read the name under the bell. Du Berge. I cleared my throat. Or, at least tried and pushed the button.

"Qui est la?"

"Je suis l'Americain." I spoke almost all I knew in French.

"Ah, oui. Yes. Yes." The door quickly swung open and my heart started to sprint. She was excited to see me.

I was suddenly excited to see her. I'd always heard of the mythical French beauties. This vision was no myth. She was gorgeous.

"Come in," she said with a thick native accent.

"Thank you," I obliged for lack of anything else to say.

"Mon package!" She took the box from me and promptly examined it; holding it first higher, then lower, turning it at different angles in front of her and me. She then put the five pound package down onto her coffee table. *"Merci beaucoup!"* She smiled at me.

"You are most welcome."

"You had a good journey? *Non?"*

"Yes."

"You must be tired. I can get you a drink?"

"Please. *S'il vous plait."* I was even more interested in Miss Du Berge than that brown rectangular pack-age at this point. The dark haired young man at JFK international airport in New York told me I would find a very alluring young lady, and as he left me, I wondered why he would want another man other than himself to carry anything so obviously important and personal to her. That cold hard knot in my stomach was still there as she handed me a glass of red wine.

"I cannot thank you so much!" She toasted me holding out her glass of wine. "Sit down, please. *Non?*"

"Thank you. Yes."

I eased down into an overstuffed yellow upholstered chair and she sat down on her matching sofa. That brown wrapped, bread-box-sized package continued to sit between us atop her coffee table.

"New York is most beautiful city. *Non?*" She looked wildly into my eyes. That cold, hard knot in my stomach was starting to heat up as it gravitated lower and lower within me.

"Yes. But not as beautiful as your country seems so far, Mademoiselle Du Berge."

"Marie."

"Marie."

"You will be staying on the Riviera for one week. *N'est ce pas?* I have your return ticket as you requested for next Sunday."

"*Oui.* Yes. I always wanted to come to the Riviera during the film festival in Cannes."

"Ah. *Oui!* Then, you are not a cinema fan. Yes?"

"Yes!" I laughed at her charm, my eyes slowly shifting from her exquisite body to that box. What the hell was in that box? I kept wondering.

"I shall take you then to Cannes tomorrow. We can see the screening of my nominated movie."

"You are an actress?"

"*Oui*. And you are an accountant."

"Your friend in New York told you."

"*Il est mon frere. Mon* brother."

"Oh."

I felt both relieved and more anxious at once. Relieved that the contact in New York was not her lover, and more anxious to find out whatever it was in that box could not be carried by her brother. Why was a Canadian Rockies skiing trip more important to him? Or, more convenient?

"He must be some avid skier," I asked more than stated, "to want to go on to Alberta, Canada himself and trust me with your package."

"*Oui. Le package.* I cannot be thanking you so much. You will enjoy your *voyage en France.*" Marie stood up and lifted that brown wrapped box off her table, leaned over and kissed me on each cheek, then quickly disappeared into her bedroom with it. My eyes travelled abruptly to her breasts when she leaned over holding that package between us. She was clad only in a short white terry cloth beach robe with a very delicate pink and white bikini becoming quite visible underneath. What had I gotten myself into?

Two

The water was beautiful. Marie had given me one of her brother, Pierre's, bathing trunks and taken me for a swim in her backyard. The Mediterranean Sea water was the same blue-green as Marie's eyes. Sunlight glistened off both the surface of the sea and Marie's silky smooth body. Her wild-eyed smile lit up the water even more.

That cold, hard knot in my body had completely warmed over. And my new French hostess must have noticed. For she swam up to me, grabbed me around the waist and pulled me under the waves. Before I knew what was happening we were making mad passionate love to each other in about three or four feet of crystal-clear salt water.

Marie slipped off first her bikini top; then together with me helped me off with my trunks. That brown wrapped package of her's swam completely out of my mind. By the time I helped her slither out of the bottom of her pink and white bikini, I thought I had figured out more why I had agreed to carry that box of hers all the way from New York to France in the first place. My accounting firm was going great. All accounts were adding up and going along smoothly. Too smoothly I figured. Boringly, in fact. I *needed* a little more excitement in my life.

Marie wrapped her arms and legs around me and started moaning and cursing in French. The waves buffeted us back and forth taking our breaths away. We rocked and came together holding onto each other for dear life. I forgot for the moment where I was and why I had come. That five pound rectangular package in her bedroom was completely forgotten.

When it was over she swam away and I followed. From thirty to thirty-five yards out we could see the majesty of the clean white sand above the cresting waves, and the scattered houses climbing up from the shore. I never thought before it could be so secluded and private at any stretch along the Riviera. Paradise *was* bliss.

THREE

"You must accompany me to dinner *ce soir,* Alain."
"Fine. Great. Where?"

"We will be dining *avec* my producer *et* film company."

"Won't I be in the way?"

"In the way?"

"You know. Would I be welcome there?"

"Oh. I see. Of course, Alain. They would be happy to be meeting with you. An *Americain.*"

"I heard the French people don't like Americans that much."

"Oh, *non?*" she radiated. "And where did you get such silly ideas?"

"I don't know," I said sheepishly shrugging my shoulders. We both let out a laugh.

She swam closer, kissed me once again and told me she'd pick me up at my hotel at six-thirty that evening.

I told her I did not really want to leave her right then. But I did still have to check into my hotel room and unpack my things before I might lose my reservations.

"*Oui. Jusque-la.*"

She smiled and waved at me; then swam away leaving me to swim back to shore and get dressed alone in her empty beach front house. I was amazed. I knew Marie Du Berge for two hours, had already made mad passionate love to her and was now trusted to swim back to her house without her to get dressed and leave.

That box came floating back to me. What was in that box? I had to know. Yet I knew I could not tamper with it and betray that trust she so obviously placed in me. It was aching me to know what was in that box.

I found her brother's bathing suit washed up on shore and quickly got into it. Why, I don't know, for nobody else was in sight; then made way to her house. I turned to wave. But she was busy swimming parallel to shore some distance out.

That package was in her bedroom. I looked out around the thin, gently blowing white drapes and through her living room window when I had finished dressing. She was still swimming parallel to the beach. Maybe I could get it open somehow without peeling any of the brown paper off with the masking tape.

I walked into her bedroom to search for the box. There it was sitting unopened on her full sized bed.

My heart started to pound against my chest. I approached the object in question carefully. Whatever was inside was packed very securely. I knew that from the start. I had accepted the package from Marie's brother, Pierre, in the airport with much curiosity.

"What is in the package?" I asked him at the terminal.

"Oh. It is just some papers with some other stuff. I would take them over myself, but I have never skied the Canadian Rockies as of yet. They tell me the skiing is like that of the Continent."

"Yes. I think so." What did I know of skiing? To me, skiing was something they did only on weekends on ABC TV's, *The Wide World of Sports.*

"I have already sent my equipment on ahead of myself and have my friends waiting there for me."

"Oh." I took the package in my hands firmly and felt its weight in my grasp. It must have been important enough. Pierre did not trust it to any commercial overnight carrier. Yet why did he trust me, a total stranger?

I took the package, now on Marie's bed, and examined the tape closely. There was absolutely no way whatsoever I could pull it away from the wrapping without disturbing it permanently. So I reluctantly placed it down in the exact same position I found it in and left to the hotel.

Four

That evening, precisely at six-thirty, Marie engineered a shining red Porche convertible up to my hotel further down the beach from her locale. Money, obviously, was no problem for the Du Berge family.

"Alain. *Allo!*"

"Hi." I smiled back at her exuberance.

"Step in."

We sped inland, up the winding road, to a rather large chalet in the foothills of the alps. The three story structure looked like it was fit for Royalty. The front lawn was landscaped and manicured with bright flowering plants of all colors lining both sides of the cement walk leading to the staircase up to the front porch. The chalet somehow reminded me more of Switzerland than what I expected to find in the south of France just above the Riviera. It made me think of her brother, Pierre's Canadian skiing venture.

"Why did your brother decide to go skiing in the Rockies instead of bringing that package I brought to you?"

"Oh. Pierre. He is always thinking of himself. Never of his family." She looked upset.

"What was in that package?" I finally decided to ask her.

"Ah. Just some papers and things. They are from my father's estate."

"Oh."

"*Oui.* He died when I was just a little girl."

"I'm sorry."

"Oh. It is all right. It was a long time ago. He died in an accident. They found his automobile in a ravine along the side *de la rue.* They said his front tire blew up."

"Blew out."

"*Qu'est ce que c'est?*"

"Blew out. Blew out. Not blew up." I idly corrected her English usage saddened by her story of grief.

"*Oui.* Momma, she took it badly at first. But the government, they took care of us."

"The government?"

"*Oui.* Yes. *Mon pere,* he was an economist in the French government. He worked for President De Gaulle *apres le guerre.*"

"Doing what?"

"I am not too sure. I know he was in Indo-China for a while."

"You French left Vietnam in 1954."

"*Je comprendre*. But some French, they stayed there."

I looked at Marie a bit differently at that point. I was about to ask why he stayed behind. Or what he was even doing there in the first place when we crossed the porch and she banged a brass knocker into one of the heavy double oak doors of the chalet.

Presently the doors swung open and the butler greeted us. "*Mademoiselle Du Berge. Priere de faire entrez-vous. Comme c'est joli recondiure vous.*"

"*Merci, Albert. C'est mon ami, Monsieur Capstein d'Amerique.*"

"*Amerique?*" He pulled back and looked at me haughtily. "Hmmm."

I shot Marie an I-told-you-so look. She just winked back at me and shrugged her shoulders, puckering toward Albert. I grabbed Marie tightly around her waist and let the butler, Albert lead us, his nose high in the air, to our host and the other guests who were already waiting for us in the dining room.

"*Mademoiselle Du Berge et ton ami, Monsieur Capstein—d'Amerique!*" Albert had to clear his throat after announcing my country of origin.

"*Allo* Marie. How do you do, Mr. Capstein?" spoke the man, smiling, at the head of the table. "Here. We are still holding your seats."

"Thank you. *Merci.*"

I felt eerily out of place as I took one of the two empty chairs toward the center of the large banquet table this host was pointing at. Marie noticed my unease as she sat in the unoccupied chair next to me.

"Jean is the producer *de nos film*, Alain. Across from you is our director, Jacques Benet *et* his wife, Francois."

"Hello." I nodded at them.

"And next to them *c'est* Robert Marcelle. He is my co-star."

"Hello." I felt a pang of jealousy when introduced to the man who probably made mad passionate love to Marie on screen. "I saw you in a French movie a few years ago, Mr. Marcelle. You played a psychopathic murderer in Paris, I think."

"*Oui.* It was my best role. I won the award for Best Actor at the festival that year."

"Yes. You were quite convincing."

"You look still convinced."

"No. No."

Everybody laughed.

"And what is it that you do?"

"Me? I'm just an accountant."

"An accountant? From America? You must be doing pretty well in New York."

"How did you know I was from New York?" Everybody seemed to look at Marie's co-star in a state of shock.

Robert looked around, then shrugged his shoulders. An accountant from America. And with a Jewish last name. Must be New York."

"Well, yes. I admit it. I *am* from New York." All the dinner guests loosened up a bit as I still felt a little awkward.

"I understand you did a favor for Marie," interjected Jean Tourneaux, the producer of their film project.

"He brought over some things *pour moi a* New York."

"Yes. I brought her a package. From her brother."

"Why did you do it? You did not know them, did you?"

"No. I did not. I don't know why. I could have afforded the airfare. I guess I just wanted a little excitement in my life. Being an accountant and living by myself—it can get a little boring at times."

"*Oui. Oui.* I suppose so."

Dinner was just being served by Tourneaux's middle-aged, heavy-set maid.

"You must taste Lucille's asparagus soup. *C'est magnifique!*"

Lucille finished ladling out my soup and I savored some.

"*Oui.* It *is magnifique!*"

"*Ah, oui,*" he exclaimed.

"Alain will be coming with me to Cannes in the morning."

"That will be some excitement for you, Mr. Capstein," Jacques Benet, the director said peering over clear-rimmed glasses. He seemed to be studying me as if he were thinking of casting me in another project of his. I wondered *what* he was thinking.

"I am sure it will be." I took another spoonful of Lucille's wonderful soup and continued to reply to him. "They make the festival seem like some kind of exotic carnival back in America."

"*Oui.* You will see for yourself then, will you not?"

Something about this director, this Jacques Benet was making me feel unsettled again. I felt he was studying me as if I were an object on a canvas. Not just another person eating supper at the same table as he was.

"Marie will take good care of you there, I am sure," said Jean, the producer, from the head of the table.

"Yes. *Oui.* I am sure." I looked at her appreciatively as she returned her wild-eyed radiance.

Lucille came back from the kitchen behind me silently pushing her serving wagon. Resting on top was a suckling roast pig clutching an apple in its mouth, surrounded by pounds of baked russet potatoes, and trailed by a casserole of string beans, okra and carrots in a thick sauce peppered with tomatoes and other unknown spices and herbs.

"Wow!" I exclaimed. "This looks delicious!"

"Yes, Mr. Capstein," spoke the producer.

"Please. Call me Allan."

"Yes then. Allan."

My discomfort was easing away somewhat as I tried to imagine what lay ahead of me the next day. Everything was very exciting to me. And mysterious. Especially my new friend, Marie Du Berge.

FIVE

Marie decided I did not need to go back to my hotel room that night. I could travel the rest of the way back along the twisting road with her, past my hotel, to her house.

"Why not," I exclaimed as she manipulated her porche down the hills to the coast drive.

"*Voila!*"

"We were talking about your father before dinner. *Votre pere.* Why he was still in Vietnam after your country left."

"*Je ne connais pas.* I do not know. Momma. She said Papa was always *un bienveillant* man. Sort of a good will ambassador. Always trying to help others. I believe he was trying to teach them better business techniques."

"That must have been risky. Staying behind like that after France granted them independence."

"I suppose. Yet you *Americains*, you came in there after then."

"Yes. We did." Memories of those ensuing war years shot past my eyes. I suddenly wondered how we ever got involved in such a senseless war over there in the first place. Semiofficially, the war for us did not start for another ten years after Marie's country officially *did* pull out. The French could not hold them. What made the United States of America so pompous and noble?

"You were not a soldier there Alain?"

"No. I was still in high school when we finally pulled out the last of our troops." I paused. "My brother was there." I thought of the last time I had seen Paul. "He never came back."

"He was killed there?" Marie's eyes suddenly seemed to glue onto the twisting ribbon of a road in front of us.

"I suppose. They never found his body." The moon must have been full that night for I remember the light wincing into my eyes as I looked out the side of the car toward the sea.

"You must not think of it, Alain. Tomorrow you will be in a fantasy land. All the cinema people. All the tourists. All the cameras."

"Cameras?"

"Oui. From the media. Everyone will be there."

"Voila!" I said.

When we arrived at her house, I anticipated another go round equal to the frolic in the Mediterranean that afternoon. Marie put her key into the door and turned the handle.

"Somebody was here *ce soir.* I always lock the door when I go away for the evening. *C'est ouvert maintenant.*"

"Ouvert?"

"It is open."

"Be careful." I didn't know what else to say.

Marie pushed the door open and slowly entered. I followed close behind. Closet doors were open, clothes strewn about. Desk drawers were dangling open in disarray between the living room and her bedroom. Marie marched straight into her bedroom and ran her fingers along the undersurface of the top of her desk just inside the slot the top drawer should normally have been occupying.

"Oh, non!" she cried.

"What?"

"Mon pere's papiers. C'est parti!" She looked at me. "They are gone."

"Call the police," I said instinctively, that cold hard knot fully back in the pit of my stomach.

"Non. I cannot do that!"

"Why not?"

"You are a very nice man, Alain. Please. Soon. You will understand."

"Understand? Understand what?" I was becoming both angry and starting to shit a brick. Though I had really nobody to be angry with other than myself, it was not entirely myself I was angry at. "What did I get myself mixed up in here with you?"

"Alain. You should leave the Riviera in the morning. Only my friends on my cinema project know who you are at this point."

"What am I involved in here?"

"Please, Alain. Do not force me to tell you now." Her pleading look at me was etched with earnestness.

"Why do you not tell him, Marie?" A voice growled out from the darkened kitchen.

"Henri Beauchamps! Why are *you* here?"

A silhouette emerged from Marie's kitchen holding a half-eaten hero sandwich in one hand, an uncorked bottle of wine in the other.

"You know the answer to that one, *mon cherie."* The emerging shadow wiped some crumbs away from his face with the back of his hand; then fixed a glassy-eyed gaze on me.

"You're *frere, Pierre?*—He did well in New York."

"Leave Alain alone. *Il est un bon homme.*"

"*Alors.* You did it with him already?"

"What is going on here?" I asked.

"You did very well, *mon ami.* Nobody followed you from the airport. *Pierre* set things up very well, Marie. *C'est Pierre?*"

"That is enough. You have what you came here for, *n'est ce pas?*"

"*Aujourd'hui.* Tomorrow is another day. *N'est ce pas?*"

"You flatter yourself, Henri."

"Do I?" He took another bite of his sandwich, wiping some more crumbs off of his lips onto his sleeve. Then he looked at me again and spoke. "Alain here, is not going *anywhere* with you in the morning. *Il maintenant connais mon visage.* He is already too involved. He will not be leaving any of us until we are finished. *N'est ce pas?*"

"Finished with what?" I mousily asked.

"They think they would leave me out of this?" he mused.

"Out of what?" I still had the guts to ask.

"You are an accountant. You know how to add up two and two?"

I did not answer. I just kept staring at him. So he continued.

"We needed Monsieur Du Berge's records from Vietnam. He was quite an entrepreneur in his day."

"What kind of an entrepreneur was he?" That cold hard knot in the pit of my stomach was starting to tear right through me.

"One who knew what people wanted. And how to get it for them." Smirking, Henri stuffed the rest of his hero sandwich into his mouth, scattering some more crumbs about his face, and took a deep swallow of the red wine he was clutching in his other fist to wash it down with.

"Drugs?" I said more than asked.

"Among other things. *N'est ce pas?*" Henri looked at Marie.

"*Je suis* so sorry, Alain. You were just supposed to carry *les papiers. Alors—*" She looked at Henri as if at a loss for words.

"What if I got caught with them?"

"*Alors.* You would be in prison, *mon ami.*" Henri's stubbled face had a look of amusement upon it. I was beginning to realize I did not like this Henri Beauchamps person too much.

"Why didn't your brother carry the papers himself instead of having to use a man like me?"

"Ah. That is a good one, *mon ami,*" spoke Henri. In the first place, her *frere, Guy,* is too well known to all the authorities. And, in the second place—"

"I asked Marie. Not you, Bozo.—Hey. Wait a minute.—I thought your brother's name was Pierre!"

"Alain. Why do you not sit down?"

"Yeah." I sat down on her sofa. She sat down upon the matching yellow chair I'd first occupied so much earlier that day. Henri helped himself to another large swallow of wine from his bottle and drifted to a chair next to the door leading to the kitchen.

"*Mon pere,* he was a businessman."

"I thought he was an economist in the French government," I said sarcastically.

"He was that too, Alain."

"Why did your brother choose me to carry your *pere's*—your father's papers? If that's what they *really* are."

"That is so simple, *mon ami,*" grunted our guest/intruder, Henri Beauchamps. "You are a dull-looking unassuming Americain accountant," he laughed. "Who would suspect *you* of anything?"

My blood started to boil. Maybe I *was* a boring accountant. But, who the hell was *this pig* in front of me to tell me I'm dull-looking?

"Look, you. Just because you spill wine from a bottle all over yourself and have crumbs all over your shirt and face—that doesn't make you any kinda good judge of anybody else's character or anything."

"He has some spunk, Marie. Maybe he *will* work out good for us for later."

"Maybe I won't be around here later."

"Maybe. If you try to leave now that would be *pour certainment.*" He belched.

"What is going on here?" I felt that wonderful dinner just hours before beginning to back up on me.

"*Alors,*" spoke Marie. "When we French knew we could not stay in Vietnam, some of our people saw the tremendous profits that could be made in other ways. If they were to be friendly to the people. Teach them business techniques."

"Like how to run drugs out of the country."

"Your friend can add *deux et deux tres bien, mon cherie.*"

"Go to hell, Henri." Something in the way Marie told him that reinforced some faith I still found myself having in her.

"This all was a very long time ago. Wasn't it?" I asked.

"*Oui.* It was. *Alors.* This operation, it became a joint French *et Americain* venture over a period of time."

"So what? I still don't understand what that has to do with anything."

"Give him some more numerals to add together, Marie."

"I don't like your pig friend here too much." I glared at him.

"You want to know more? Then tell him. Tell him about his long lost missing-in-action older *Americain* brother."

"What?" My body and head just went bonkers.

"Paul Capstein. International—how you say?—*business entrepreneur."*

Six

Yesterday I stepped off an airplane and walked down into paradise. But last night hell froze over the same turf. I could not think straight anymore. My long lost, just about given up for dead, older brother, Paul was now supposedly alive and well. Or, at least, alive. The last time I *did* see him alive I was fourteen years old.

Paul was in an army uniform. I remember it as if it were yesterday. Dad pulled the car up in front of the apartment house. He honked the horn twice. Mom was there trying to shove a tin of some cookies she'd just baked for him into Paul's hands.

"Come on, Mom. I can't take these."

"They're your favorite. Chocolate chip."

"Give 'em to Allan. He loves 'em."

"You give some to your bunk mates, Paully."

"OK, Mom."

Paul reluctantly took the box and hugged her.

"Don't worry about me, Mom. I'll be back home soon." Tears started to trickle down Mom's cheeks. "Take care of my stamp collection for me. Huh, Allan?"

"Yeah. Sure, Paul. Thanks!"

We shook hands and Paul threw the tin of cookies onto the front seat of Dad's Buick and climbed in next to him.

"See ya."

He waved as Dad drove him off to the airport. That was almost—what?—twenty years ago. I never could quite accept the apparent fact of his death completely. Now, I could not imagine why I could not have accepted that fact.

"Alain. You do not look well?"

"How do you expect me to look after last night?"

"I am so sorry, Alain. I did not know how nice a man you—"

"Stop apologizing to me. You can't be so sorry. You set me up for all of this somehow." All of what I still could not figure out. Or how. "Where is that pig friend of yours this morning?"

"Henri is no friend of mine, Alain. He is—how you say?—He is the grandson *de mon pere's conspirateur*. Henri is just in this for the money."

"In *what?*" My numb brain started to spin again. "Supplying the West with enough poppy to—" I sank back down into the living room sofa where I'd just spent a miserable sleepless night.

"Can I fix you some breakfast, Alain?"

"What?" I rubbed my eyes and looked slowly up to her. She was still very sexy and alluring. No matter what had happened or taken place last night with her associate—or whatever he was—in the living room. "Why not?" I replied mostly to myself still too numb to think straight.

"You do not like pancakes with bacon?"

"Yes. I do like pancakes with bacon."

Despite it all, Ms. Marie Du Berge was still charming, innocent and attractive to me. I think I managed a smile at her.

"Then. *Voila!*"

She hurried into her kitchen, minus the intruder of last night, Henri Beauchamps, and proceeded to whip up some most delicious French pancakes, bacon and coffee.

"How did Pierre—or Guy—or whatever—"

"Guy."

"How did he get me to answer that advertisement to bring that package to you?"

"You like your crepes? *N'est ce pas?*"

"How did he—you—do it?"

"You use a computer at your office. *N'est ce pas?*"

I did not answer her.

"*Mon frere*, Guy, he broke into your office late one night and altered your spreadsheet programs." She seemed so innocent. So pure. "Every time you pressed the enter key a subliminal message flashed across your screen. You saw a picture of yourself on the beach at Cannes. And the exact copy of the ad highlighted in the newspaper with the date it would appear."

"You bastards!"

"Alain. You will see things differently soon. I am sure."

"Where is my brother, Paul?"

"*Monsieur* Capstein is somewhere in Paris."

"He *is alive?*"

"He is very much alive, Alain. He suggested the subliminal message on your computer. It was his idea. His plan. His desire to fetch you *ici.*"

"What is going on here, Marie? I've got a right to know now."

"*Oui.* You do. Your brother—Monsieur Capstein— He did not want us to tell you. He wanted to make his presence known to you only at the end. Next week in Cannes."

"Tell me, Marie. Now," I demanded gently.

"First. You must know that what we are doing is for the *end* to aggression. Not as Henri would lead you to think." She noticed my empty coffee cup and poured me a refill. "When we were leaving Vietnam, you *Americains* came to take over for us. *Mon Pere,* he wanted the people to be able to defend themselves against the Marxists. He knew how we French could not stop them. And he thought you *Americain* soldiers would meet the same fate." I kept searching her eyes over my steamy cup of coffee. *"Mon Papa.* He thought if he could train them in Western ways: teach them business skills, free market enterprising—"

"Drug running."

"Please, Alain. Allow me!"

"Go ahead."

"There *was* some drugs involved. *Mais, alors.* That got in the way later. It could not be helped."

I kept listening. Was Marie that naive? Or, was I? To keep believing in her innocence. I could not stop thinking how we first met; and hit it off. And how wide open and unprotected she kept that package on her bed when I delivered it. She kept talking.

"Some of his students, they started to supply drugs to your soldiers. *Pour mon Papa* to stay in operation, he had to overlook this business. He kept setting up businesses *dans les villages* and began setting up exporting concerns."

"Drugs."

"Non. Non! Rubber. Rice. Furniture. Drugs he could not control. Some of his partners and others he set up

began trading in drugs. Mamma, she said he resisted them at first. *Mais les Americains,* they told him to look a *l'autre direction."*

"The Americans told him that."

"Oui. They were far from home. The war was tough on them. Your officers, they overlooked drug usage. *Mon Pere* was correct. The only way to defeat Marxism was not a military one. That was why he decided to stay behind there. And decided to go along and to look the other way at first."

I found myself believing all she had to say. Except for one thing.

"What does Paul—my brother—have to do with all of this?"

"Your *frere,* Paul Capstein worked *avec mon pere.* He was shot down behind North Vietnamese lines." That I knew. The rest was brand new to me. "He was found and wound up being protected by a family in a Cambodian village. He was hooked on drugs. Heroine. The Cambodians, they gave it to him whenever he needed it. Soon, he saw how *les Americains* were running drugs there. He got involved in this operation. *Monsieur* Capstein. He wanted to tell you *tout*—everything— himself."

"So. He's a drug dealer. Huh?" I shoved my remaining pancakes and bacon away from myself. "No wonder he never came back!"

"*Non. Non*, Alain. *Monsieur* Capstein, he tried to stop *les Americains*. He went along with it only so he could try to stop *l'operation*. He wanted to tell you everything. This is why he never could come home *a* New York again."

"I like you, Marie."

"*Oui*."

"*Oui*." I could not believe what was coming out of my mouth. "This story." I grappled for the words. "I do not understand.—"

"*Ton frere*, he wanted to see you. He wanted you to know he was still alive."

"Paul was a good man." I winced with pain. What had happened to him I could not even begin to imagine.

"*Oui*. He still is a good man. When this week is all over, Monsieur Capstein will be able to go back to New York again *avec tu*."

"When *what* is all over? I still can't—don't—understand."

"I am so sorry, Alain. *Ton frere*. Monsieur Capstein. He would not allow me to tell you any more."

My head kept swimming.

"He will tell you himself."

SEVEN

The water alternately in front and to the left of us sparkled like so many emeralds, diamonds and pearls as Marie Du Berge drove us quickly along the winding shore drive into the heart of Cannes. The brilliant crystal blue sky above paled into the sea's edge. Not a single wisp of a cloud intruded to blemish the horizon. Nature was playing a cruel hoax on me.

"When will I get to see Paul?" I felt turned inside-out. My insides were ablaze. Being consumed by anger. And fear. My skin was moist from sweat. Brought out by the raging inferno inside. My head was still busy swimming—practically drowning—in its encasement.

"I will try to have Jean contact him when we get to *l'hotel*. Henri was not supposed to know you were coming this week. We told him you were to arrive *next month*. We did not want him to know *ton frere's true* wishes."

I kept staring straight ahead at the twisting ribbon of a road in front of us. All I could see was Paul's face. He would not look the same. Funny. I still had his stamp collection at home. I never got rid of it. I'd always noticed how he'd had a penchant for European stamps over United States issues. I wondered if he still collected them any more.

"Do not worry so much. It is not so terrible as you may think," I heard Marie's voice say.

"Are you for real? Two days ago I thought I was taking off for the biggest adventure of my life," the words stuck in my throat. "Only to find out I'd been manipulated by you. And my—my missing-in-action older brother. You know, I still have his stamp collection. He asked me to hold onto it for him. That was almost—what?—twenty years ago!"

"*Ici.* We will call him together. *Non?*"

We'd just pulled up in front of the *L'Hotel des Ors* along the broad palm tree-lined main boulevard in the heart of Cannes. It *was* a fairy tale setting. Just as I had always dreamed it to be.—Or, at least, must have seen it on my computer!—Marie left the car in front of the hotel and handed her keys to the valet.

"*Oui. Merci, Mlle. Du Berge!*" He recognized her instantly. I had almost forgotten she was a national celebrity in France.

"Merci, Monsieur." She smiled at him and walked up the white stairsteps, across the spotless plaza and into the lobby. "Come on, Alain!"

I followed close behind. Marie walked briskly through the lobby past the concierge's desk straight to the bank of elevators in the back along the left hand wall. I scarcely noticed the casino off to the right or the entrance to the main showroom just before the three elevators.

"Ici." she smiled at me as I stepped into the first red and gold carpeted elevator just behind her. I had no reason to blame myself for any of this anymore. So I did not. The burning in my guts just got hotter as the operator lifted us to the top level.

We exited the elevator and I followed Marie down the corridor. At room 614, Mlle. Du Berge stopped and gently knocked on the door.

"Jean Tourneaux," I sarcastically greeted him.

"You are not happy to see me, *Monsieur* Capstein?"

"Henri Beauchamps showed up at my home last night, Jean."

"Oh," he looked at the floor and grimaced. "Come on in then. Why don't you?

"How do you like the Riviera here *Monsieur* Capstein?" he asked after we stepped in.

"Fine. I thought you lived in your own chalet last night."

"Ah, yes. I always take this suite during the festival. It is so much more convenient for all the activities."

"Yeah. Great.—What's happening? Where is my brother?"

"Your brother? What does he know so far, Mar—?"

"Enough to know my brother is still alive!"

"Your brother is a very brave man, *Monsieur* Capstein. He is a hero."

"Where is he? I wanna see him. If he *is alive!*"

"You do not wish to speak to him. Do you?"

"Call him up. Now!" I was amazed at my forcefulness.

"Un minute. S'il vous plait." Jean Tourneaux walked over to a desk and picked up the receiver to a very elegant white enameled, gold trimmed French style telephone.

"Oui. Paris, s'il vous plait . . . 012237 . . . Oui . . . Merci beaucoup . . ." Tourneaux stared at me. Studying me plaintively. Marie delved into my eyes with sympathy. I really did still like her.

"Allo . . . Monsieur Capstein? . . . Oui . . . Yes. I did . . . He is fine . . . Fine . . . He is right here standing in my room with me . . . I am so sorry. *Je comprende . . .* I know . . . *Oui . . . Non . . . Non . . .*Henri Beauchamps found out he was here with Marie and

he . . . *Oui* . . . I do not know what he said to him . . ."
He looked at me; then at Marie.

"Ne trop pas, Jean."

"Not too much Marie tells me . . . *Oui* . . . *Oui* . . ."
Jean put his hand over the receiver. *"Monsieur*
Capstein. Your brother wishes to speak to you."

My heart started pounding in my ears. I forgot everything. Where I was. How I got there. I took the receiver and put it to my ear.

"Hello?"

"Hello Allan."

"Paul?"

"Yes. This is Paully." The voice sounded different.
There was a huskiness that I never heard before when
I still knew him.

"How do I know this is you?"

"You still have my stamp collection, Allan?"

"Yeah." I was dumbfounded.

"Did you keep it up, or what?"

It was my brother, Paully all right. His sense of humor seemed the same.

"Not really. I did at first. Then I sorta lost interest
in it when you were reported missing-in-action."

"Yeah. I know." The voice on the other end of the
line dropped somewhat. "How's Mom and Dad?"

"They moved to Florida. Dad sold the deli about
six, seven years ago."

"I know. I got some people. They keep me up on these things."

"Paully. Why the hell—What the heck is going on here? Why the hell didn't you at least—You were supposed to be dead for a long time."

"I wish I coulda told you sooner, Allan."

"What? Told me what? I heard you were into dealing drugs? Why couldn't you at least let us know you were alive?"

"I'm sorry, Allan. I wish I could of. I really do. I'd like to see ya, kid."

"When? I wanna see ya too."

"Tonight. You are with Marie?"

"Marie?" I looked at her. "Yes. I'm with Marie."

"Good. She is a good kid."

"I know." I heard the words coming out of my mouth.

"Let her show you a good time until I can get down there."

"Yeah. Thanks Paully. I mean—"

"See ya tonight, Allan. At Marie's place."

"OK."

"See ya tonight."

The line went dead. I stood there holding the receiver in front of me, expecting the alarm clock to sound and wake me up.

EIGHT

The rest of the day passed in a haze. I kept seeing my brother in his uniform standing in front of me. He was drafted right after graduating from college. Paully could have avoided the draft. He could have gone up to Canada. Or into teaching as so many of his friends did at that time to beat the draft. But he chose to do his country's duty. To "get in and get out and get it over with." He would not look the same clean-cut older brother I was looking at through the haze that brilliantly sunlit afternoon. His raspier voice was cluing me in on that. I still saw his bright infectious smile clearly. How, I did not know.

"Alain. You must take in *le view de le gulf* from *le chateau* atop Mount Chevalier."

"Yeah." I kept looking at Paully across the Mediterranean.

"*C'est tout magnifique!*"

I felt her smile on me and I turned to look at her.

"You are a beautiful young woman, Marie."

"*Merci.*"

She grabbed the stick shift and changed gears as we started to climb the mountain. The haze in my eyes steadily lifted as we climbed higher and higher. Soon, all I could see clearly was the young lady next to me in the driver's seat.

"Have you ever been to America?"

"*Oui.* When I was a little girl. *Ma mere,* my mother, she took me and my brother to Washington. We stayed with a family of diplomats."

"Listen. I really don't know too much about what the heck is going on here yet. But I do know for some reason I still trust you."

"*Merci.*"

"Stop the thank yous and apologies already." I smiled at her.

Marie pulled off to the side of the road and shut her motor upon arriving at the top of Mount Chevalier.

"It is *tout magnifique* up here," I said as I looked around.

She got out of her porche on her side of the car and I exited my side. I was now able to feel the warm breeze and hot sun on my skin as we walked along in silence to a lookout point high above the gulf.

"Those islands down there once belonged to an ancient civilization. They still bear their name. *Les Lerins isles.*" I stared out being soothed by her gentle voice. "This chateau behind us *est le Chateau des Abbes de Lerins. C'est* where *le* town *de* Cannes originally began."

"Why are you telling me all this?"

I looked out over the water watching the pleasure boats and the fishing boats float along. She grabbed my hand and I instinctively grabbed her around the waist. I turned and we kissed—gently at first—soon running our tongues together inside each others' mouths. Suddenly I felt everything—whatever everything was going to be—was going to be all right.

"You are like this with all Americans you meet?"

"Only those who come to me so shyly carrying packages from America."

"What was in that box, Marie? Exactly."

"You will see your brother tonight."

"I know."

"I will show you. Come. Let us go home."

She took my hand and led me back to her Porche.

"Let me drive back."

"You can drive a stick shift?"

"*Oui.*"

She threw me the keys. I jumped in and we took off back down the mountain and the winding ribbon of a road. She told me where to turn. And we were back at her house.

She took my hand once again in front of her door and led me in across her threshold. Marie wasted no time going to her desk where she took out that large manila envelope Henri left behind, all dishevelled, in the kitchen last night. Inside that straightened-out envelope was what had gotten me here.

"Alain. There is much here. It is both—good and not so good. Do not judge anything until you are finished looking at all of it."

My heart started to race again. That cold hard knot in the pit of my stomach started to ache. I took the manila envelope and slowly unlaced its strings. Marie stood by anxiously.

I opened the flap of the maroon envelope and looked inside. I reached in and took out a stack of legal sized file folders. Each had a description of sorts written across its top. I glanced at Marie; and then thumbed through them.

One of them caught my eye immediately. It was marked: CAPSTEIN, PAUL B. 1971—1978.

"Do not judge too hastily Alain."

I opened it and started to read:

Capstein, Paul B.
Born: August 8, 1948
United States Army: Rank—Captain

—Shot down over Cambodia September 18, 1972
—Ran drugs between Cambodia and Saigon: December 1972 to October 1973
—Disappeared October 4, 1973
—Located by CIA in Marseilles, France: April 1978
—Protected by French government

I carefully thumbed through the remaining folders. No more were marked Capstein.

"What happened between 1978 and today?"

"You're *frere, Monsieur* Paul Capstein. He worked with *mon pere* in Vietnam. He wanted to expose the drug operation. This is why he could never come home to you. The CIA was too involved. If he tried to come home or contact you, he would be killed. *Mon Papa*, he set your *frere* up—Did I say it right?—"

"*Oui.* I think."

"He set your *frere* up in Marseilles. As long as *Monsieur* Capstein kept quiet and stayed away from home they would leave him to himself. If he came home to you they thought he would say something to you. The CIA had enough troubles back in America in those days they tell me."

"Whoa."

"Your brother has been working for an international antiterrorist organization. We still do importing and exporting with Vietnam. But that is mostly separate from our other activities."

I was beside myself. I looked down at Marie and myself—holding Paully's folder in my hands—now floating outside my desensitized body, speechless.

"Come back down to earth, Alain." Marie took my skinny wrist in her firm yet feminine fingers. "It is not so terrible. Soon. He will be able to go back to New York *avec tu.* You will see."

"I guess so."

"You will soon know. *Pour certainment.*"

Marie kept smiling at me and I felt myself slowly come back down and reenter my very novocained body.

"Come. We will go for a swim. *N'est ce pas?*"

"*Oui,*" I said instantly. "With or without our bathing suits?"

"It is your choice."

"Come. *Ici,*" I demanded. I grabbed her by her waist and we helped each other into our birthday suits as she proceeded to flush the novocaine from my body. The Mediterranean would have to wait for us.

NINE

A round five o'clock that sun drenched afternoon I began to get anxious again. I woke up next to Marie lying naked on the sand. She was exquisite. Not only was she one of the most beautiful girls I'd ever seen; she was one of the strongest. Her innocent sparkling eyes hid all that she knew and was involved in. I nudged her right arm gently and she opened her precious eyes and rolled onto her side; then slid on top of me.

"Oh God!" I exclaimed as she put her hand between my legs.

"It is not good?"

"It is *tres bien!*"

"*Voila!*" She took my rising member and made me forget about my brother and any terrorists again.

I soon rolled her over onto her back and completed what she had initiated this time.

"I think I could fall in love with you Mlle. Du Berge," I said when we were through.

"I would not object, *Monsieur* Alain Capstein."

"Come. Let us put some clothes back on our bodies."

"You are sure?"

"My brother will soon be here. No?"

"*Oui.*" She sounded disappointed.

"*Oui.*" I got up and took her hand. I helped her up and we walked unclad, slowly back to her beachhouse. A few sea gulls flew overhead, oblivious to us, searching along the shoreline for their supper. One bird swooped down on an unsuspecting clam and carried him high up into the gentle breeze; then dropped him down to the firmer sand just above the softly laping waves. This caused his hard shell to break wide open. Instantly several of the more oportunistic sea gulls converged, stealing its meat contents away from the high flying gull. The scene reminded me of one I'd seen earlier on the Lower East Side of New York. I was in my car with a girlfriend one evening, on our way to an off-off-Broadway theater. Some guy got out of a taxi in front of us carrying a large brown paper bag. He stood in the center of the street and held it up high over his head. Suddenly, out of nowhere, hundreds of street people converged upon him completely blocking our path. He was the local drug pusher apparently arriving a little later than usual or desired that particular evening with the goodies.

"Your brother will be very happy to see you."

"How well do you know my brother?"

"*Monsieur* Capstein is like a father to me. When he came to Paris he would always come to our house and bring me presents. When *mon pere* died he handled most of the funeral arrangements."

"How *did* your father die?"

"I told you all I know. One morning he was found in his auto in a ravine off the side of a road in the country-side with his tire blown up."

"Who killed him? You don't think it was an accident, do you?" I held her back door open for her.

"Put your pants on, Alain."

That anxious feeling was coming back. Suddenly, we heard the hum of an automobile coming closer and closer. I hitched up my white pants and buttoned my shirt up to mid-chest level, stepping into my tan loafers and walked up to the front door. Pulling into the side of the drive was a yellow convertible Peugeot. The driver had short cropped grey hair covering half of his head and a full salt and pepper beard covering his face. The face belonged to my dad. The smile slowly growing through the camouflage on his face belonged to my long-lost, almost given up for dead older brother, Paul. I involuntarily took a few faint steps toward him as he stepped out of his car.

"Paully?"

"Hi, Allan." He stood calmly at the car door watching me, gaging my reaction, I guess.

"You look like Dad."

"Oh yeah? Thanks."

He started to come toward me.

"I'm looking at a ghost!"

"Oh yeah?"

At that point we stood two or three feet apart looking at each other through tear-filled eyes; then, suddenly, we hugged each other for the first time in at least twenty years.

"You look good, Allan."

"Yeah." I could not stop shaking.

"You look good," he repeated.

Paul finally broke the embrace a bit.

"How's Mom?"

"She's fine. She's fine. She likes it a lot down in Florida." I tried to stop shaking. I wiped some moisture away from my cheeks.

"I've been told."

"Paully. Where the hell have you been for so long? What the hell has been happening with you all these years?" We were still holding each other by our arms.

"Not so much."

"*What?*"

"Calm down, Allan."

"Why? *How? Why?*"

"*Bon soir*, Marie."

"*Bon soir, Monsieur* Capstein." She was standing by the door watching quietly, dressed in a pair of peach colored stretch pants, I think.

"Why don't we go inside and try to catch up on things?"

"Yeah." What else could I say?

"Marie is like a daughter to me, Allan."

"So she's been telling me." She looked over to me warmly and smiled. I might have smiled back to her as well. But I was too overwhelmed and discircuited by my brother's sudden reappearance to realize exactly what I was saying or doing that particular moment.

"I trust she is taking good care of you?"

"That she is. That she is." This time I am sure I did smile back at her.

"Marie. Why don't you fix us a couple a drinks for ourselves?" I half-expected him to ask for a martini. Shaken. Not stirred. "What will you have, Allan?"

"Me? I don't—I'll have a scotch and soda, I guess."

"That's what Dad always usta have."

"Yeah. I know." I felt my eyes mist up again as I looked at my long-separated older brother.

"I'll take the same, Marie. *S'il vous plait.*"

"*Oui, Monsieur* Capstein." She spun around and went into her kitchen.

"I understand you turned out to be some kind of a good businessman, kid."

"I guess. I'm doing all right."

"I hear you've got one a the most prestigious accounting firms in New York."

"I'm doing all right I guess."

"You've still got that modesty you always used to have."

"I don't know."

"Ya remember that time I was taking economics in college and I hadda invest an imaginary thousand dollars in the stock market at the beginning of the course; then try to make the most profit by the end a the course? You gave me all the advice on what to buy and sell? If I'd a listened to you all the way I'd a gotten an automatic A in the course for making a $4,300 profit in three and a half months instead a just breakin' even."

"Yeah. I do remember that."

"Remember what you said when I told my professor about you and your advice, and he said he'd like to use you as his stock broker?"

"No. What did I say?"

"What's the big deal? All you have to do is read the paper an' make lucky guesses."

"Yeah. That *is* all that it is. Isn't it?" The missing twenty years between us just seemed to have vanished into thin air. "I told you to buy into that cable TV company based down in Texas. Remember?"

"Yeah. I do. How were you so sure a that?"

"That was easy. Lady Bird Johnson just bought up a big percentage of that stock. I couldn't see it *not* making a big jump on the Board. The other one you didn't wanna listen to me on was that helicopter manufacturer. They still needed all those new helicopters in the war then."

"Yeah." Paully looked away a few seconds. The missing years between us suddenly sprang up again.

"What happened to you, Paully? Why couldn't you at least of contacted us in all this time?"

Marie just came back into the living room with our mixed drinks.

"I understand you met Henri Beauchamps the other day here." Paul looked at Marie. "What did he tell him?"

"Not that much. He made us sound like drug lords."

"Ah. Henri. Henri is a bum. He thinks differently than most people."

"I'm not really too interested in Henri Beauchamps, Paul. I need—I wanna know what's been going on with you. I saw a folder about ya after you were shot down. It said you were involved with drugs, Paully."

"The war was rotten, Allan. Worse than you could imagine. We used to bomb empty rice patties on orders just to say we bombed. All the while our guys were bein' knocked off on the ground by snipers or ambush attacks. We'd go back to our barracks or positions and hear what was goin' on back in the States. The antiwar demonstrations. They were goin' on before I shipped out. How we were bein' called baby killers."

"Yeah."

"After a few months we'd begin countin' the weeks—the days—we'd be comin' back home. Then, after a time, we'd wonder how would life be—when we got back home. How would we be treated by everybody?"

"What's this got to do with—"

"Drugs were all over the place. It was easy. Get high and forget what the hell you were doing there in the first place. The longer you'd be there—the more and more difficult it was to come up with any kinda answer to that question. Even the most gung ho guys at boot camp—they didn't know what the hell they were doin' over there after a while. I tried heroine one day after I was there a few months. It seemed like a good thing to do. I got hooked, Allan. I was having a blast for a while. I didn't give a crap about anything after that except gettin' high. Then one day I got shot down behind enemy lines. In Cambodia. It was great. They took care of me. The Cambodians. Gave me food and shelter."

"And drugs?"

"Yeah." Paully looked into the distance enigmatically. "An' drugs." Paully looked around unfocused; then slowly focused down deeply into his scotch and soda in his hand and took a shot. "I thought at that point I finally had the whole thing figured out. The war was about drugs. We were running drugs through Cambodia to Saigon, then to the West. I finally thought I had a reason to be there. It was great while I was still freaked out. I was flyin' poppy and I was gettin' good money too.

"Then one day the inevitable happened. I smacked up the copter on the way back from a run and wound up havin' to go cold turkey in the middle a nowhere. A week-and-a-half later I found myself back near our landing strip somehow. The Cambodians found me strung out in the middle a the jungle."

Paully looked at the empty ice-cubed glass in his hand and shook it around in a circular motion.

"I will fill it for you, *Monsieur* Capstein."

"*Oui*, Marie."

She took the glass from my brother's hand and took it into the kitchen with her. Then my brother continued his story.

"While I was recovering, layin' there in one of their huts, I started to think, 'What the hell am I *doing* here? This ain't too great!' I stopped taking the junk. I kept flyin' though. I didn't want 'em to know I was straight. I was gonna blow the whistle. Turn 'em all in.—But I couldn't."

"Why not?"

"They were mostly CIA. When they realized what I might be up to they tried to shut me up. At first, they tried to buy my silence. I played along with it. Took their money. But they didn't trust me anymore.

"Marie's father worked with lots a their suppliers, the poppy farmers. He helped sneak me outta the country. Before he got me out, they let me know not to say anything or to go home again. They know how to keep your tongue silenced, Allan."

"Why couldn't you at least of—" I stopped myself in the middle of my stupid question.

"They woulda started on the delicatessen. They woulda burned it down. They let me know that. All your phones were tapped. They still are. If I tried to call any a ya—it would of been the last you woulda hearda me."

"Then why did they leave you alone after they located you in France?"

"Five years later? By the time they found me I was working for the French. *Monsieur* Du Berge had lots of connections. Besides, we were having too many problems with the Arabs and OPEC at the time."

"Yeah. We still are. But—"

"I had a lotta combat and intelligence experience, Allan. Europe was faced with an even greater threat and problem with the Arabs and OPEC than the U.S."

"Yeah." I guessed he was right.

"I started working undercover for the French—trying to infiltrate their Mid-East organizations. Wanna know why the Iranians released all those embassy workers they took the day Ronald Reagan took office as President, by the way?"

"Why?"

"Never mind the Iran-Contra affair. That was only part of it. The real reason was they thought he was gonna blow 'em off the face of the map if they didn't shake a leg quick enough. Nuke 'em. They made a wise decision, Allan."

"Oh yeah?"

"Yes, little brother." Paul took a slug of his fresh scotch and soda. "They sometimes use a great deal of common sense, those Arabs." He flashed a vague smile.

"Marie told me you'd be able to come home soon, Paully."

"You weren't supposed to know anything for another week. Henri Beauchamps screwed that up the other night."

"Why did you want me to stay a whole week before I was supposed to know you were even alive, Paully? Marie told me how you got me over here."

"Yeah. Great idea. Wasn't it? Putting subliminal messages into your computers." Paully's sense of humor was showing again.

"Yeah. Pretty good." I had to admit it.

"I wanted you to relax. Enjoy yourself for a while. See the festival."

I couldn't immediately tell if he was kidding or not.

"Who is this Henri Beauchamps character?"

"Henri. Henri Beauchamps' father helped me out of Nam with *Monsieur* Du Berge. They snuck me out through East Germany; then through the French Embassy into West Berlin. From there I flew to Paris. Henri grew up to be an arms merchant. For the right price he is also an antiterrorist. He is an embarrassment to his father."

"Paully. Could you tell me what is going on here or not yet?"

"We've become an independent ideological organization. Part of our activities is to make sure of the balance of power in various parts of the world." I kept listening, noticing how relaxed I was becoming with all of this. "We have a problem with Iraq. As long as their leader, Saddam Hussein, thinks he's powerful enough, he keeps his terrorist groups pretty quiet. Only, he's getting *too* strong lately. We have reason to believe he's close to having nuclear power. And is preparing to use it on his Arab neighbors so he can take control of the world oil market. He already is preparing to march into Kuwait to his south."

"What do you have to do with all of this, Paully?"

"Henri and I sold him lots a his weapons and equipment. We were interested in helping him defeat Iran a few years ago to keep the Ayatollah in check."

"You sound like you are working for the CIA."

"*With* the CIA, Allan. *With* the CIA. Not everything they do is bad. When this week is over, the world might be a little better off and never even know it. Henri thinks we are gonna sell this Hussein character the missing element to his nuke pile. That's why he thinks he can get away with invading Kuwait."

"What are you gonna do?"

"We're gonna be settin' him up for a hit. Prevent the whole invasion in the first place. With Henri's unwitting help."

My brother *was* a hero, I thought.

"When it's over, the CIA says they're willing to overlook old times an' let me come back into the States again. They are a tough lot." Paully's teeth flashed through his salted and peppered face again. "Their ex-boss is now the president over there. He's gonna let me in after this as long as I keep my mouth shut— Don't say anything or mention anybodies' names to anybody about their Vietnam days."

"Mom and Dad are gonna be shocked."

"Yeah."

TEN

We talked all night, Paully and myself. Marie went to sleep early as my brother and I caught up on old times. Or at least tried our best to catch up. We began at the point of our separation.

"You used to wanna be an engineer, or architect or something, didn't you?" I asked my older brother.

"Yeah. Somethin' like that. I wanted to design things. Cars. Buildings. I don't know."

"Why didn't you try to get out of the draft?"

"What for? Go up to Canada? Teach in the ghetto? Nah. I figured I'd get in an' get out quick. Get it all over with. I figured hey, I got a free education at CCNY—"

"City College—"

"Yeah. We must of been in Vietnam for *some* good reason. I'll pay 'em back for the free education."

"Everybody was taking over campus buildings protesting the war back then."

"No. Not everybody. Half the students sympathized *for* the war."

"Yeah," I paused. "I wonder. How many a them didn't fight the draft?"

"The garbage. All those that go gung ho over war, but do everything they can not to risk their own asses in battle. You see 'em all the time. All B.S. and no guts."

"Sounds like our current Vice-President."

"Yeah. The 'boy scout'. Don't worry about him too much. He'll never get elected straight out on his own."

"Yeah. I think you're right about that."

"How come you never got married yet in all this time, Al?" My brother's teeth started to glow through his facial foliage again.

"I don't know. Guess I been too busy running the company. I haven't had the free time to think of settling down." My mind switched to that beautiful young lady I'd just recently met, sleeping in the next room. "How bout you? You musta come in contact with some pretty interesting women in all this time."

"Well. There *is* someone I'd like you to meet. In Paris, kid."

"Your wife?"

"We never took the vows. If that's what you're askin'."

ELEVEN

The next morning I woke up abruptly, startled to see my father shaking me to consciousness.

"Allan. Let's go."

"Dad?" My eyes slowly focused on the face over my head.

"Rise and shine!"

"Paully?" I rubbed my eyes. "Shit. Thought you were Dad."

"Thought you were Mom."

I threw on my pants and staggered into the kitchen to witness Marie doing her usual thing. Preparing a delicious breakfast.

"You slept good last night. *Non?*"

"*Oui.* Not long enough. But good." I dreamt of when I used to watch Paully and his friends play basketball together at the center on weekends when we were growing up.

"You two seem to of hit it off well, I see."

"Oui. Ton frere, il est un bon homme."

"Oui. T'il aimerais?"

"Oui. J'aime lui."

"What?"

"She says she likes you."

"Oui. Je like her too." I smiled at her as she placed a filled powdered plate of crepes in front of me.

"We're going into Cannes today," Paul said while helping himself to a mouthful of crepes that Marie placed in front of him. "I have to arrange a few things with our *bon ami,* Henri Beauchamps."

"Oh yeah?"

"He knows the so-called arms deal with Hussein would have to be set probably this week now that you are here. Not next month as we wanted him to think. We're gonna use him to try to bring Hussein out in the open. Then pop him."

I felt Marie's and my brother's eyes upon me as I could taste the last forkful of crepes coming back up to my throat.

"Why did you get me over here now, Paully?" I asked putting down my fork. "You don't need me for any of this."

He looked at Marie and then answered.

"Number one. Guy could not be seen carrying any-thing onto any European bound airplane without chancin' being intercepted by any Mid-East Arab terrorist organization. They are all aware this Saddam guy is close to having nuclear weapons. And they all know we've been talkin' to him, and have dealt arms to him in the past. Any one a them would like to get their hands on the detonating devices for those weapons. Then they could negotiate a deal with any madman they wanted a. Guy took another package with him to Canada two hours before your plane boarded for Nice to lead anybody interested astray."

"What if they knew I was carrying your package?"

"Nothing woulda happened to ya. Didn't you notice all the French servicemen on the airplane with ya?"

"Yeah. As a matter of fact I did. There were two a them sitting in the same row next to me."

"And three in fronna ya. They weren't soldiers. They were from our organization. Nobody was gonna get close to ya. The taxi driver from the airport? He was one a ours. You were well in hand."

"I still don't understand. What kinda papers were so important in that box? And, why couldn't you wait another week to see me if they're gonna let you come back to the U.S? You could not of found another courier, Paully?"

"The rest of those papers: they were mostly records of some of our clandestine operations. All our arms sales were in there. Who bought what. When. How much. What method they paid for it. Where we got our hands on it. Also some of our antiterrorist information and activities going back to before *Monsieur* Du Berge—Marie's father—died. We needed those papers here in a safer place. For obvious reasons. At best they could be a huge embarrassment for us. At worst, many of our undercover agents would be found out and put to rest."

My brother's sly sense of humor still shone through. I was too dumbstruck to feel shocked.

"Why we used you, Allan? That was my doing completely. They hinted I could go back home before. Things didn't pan out. Back in '86 they told me: I get them Noriega, they'll cut me some slack about coming back home."

"They *got* Noriega. *What happened?*"

"They got restless. Didn't give us a chance. Decided they'd rather invade the place first. Flex their muscles. Make heroes outta themselves on the nightly news and get the dreaded drug dealer themselves in fronna the world."

"Yeah."

"I really think they balked because the VP wanted a be president a year or so down the road an' didn't want any shadows from the past showing up at the wrong time."

I sat there listening to him. My head was spinning like a top. "I voted for him." I didn't know what else to say.

"See what ya did?"

They say people change with time. I know that's true. But, as much as Paul changed from when I remembered him when I was a fourteen-year-old kid, something deep inside him I could sense still remained the same. That same something that always made me look up to him. I could almost put my finger on it.

"You see Mom an' Dad lately?"

"Yeah. I was down there a couple a months ago. Mom likes it down there a little more than Dad, I think. I think Dad misses some a the grittiness of the city."

"He grew up in Brownsville. Whata ya expect?"

"I don't know. Most of the guys he grew up with there wound up dead or in prison. How do you *miss* that?" I found the strength to take another bite of my half-eaten pancakes and another sip of orange juice.

Paully cut himself a rather large mouthful of Marie's crepes and stuffed his mouth with it. Then he washed it down with a huge gulp of her coffee. He wiped his beard and lips and then dug in for some more of the fine eatery.

"Dad usta make the pickles himself for the delicatessen. Remember?" I wistfully switched the subject.

"Yeah." Paully laughed. "Usta stink up the whole basement. He usta *smell* from pickles."

"Mom thought he was nuts. So did I for a while."

Paul looked up at me.

"What changed your mind?"

"Every time my friends would come by for a sandwich on a Saturday or Sunday. They'd always ask for an extra pickle. Dad wouldn't think twice. He'd say, 'Here. Have another pickle,' like he was doing them a big favor or somethin'. Making a big sacrifice. An he'd always give it to 'em. I thought it was funny. Them getting free pickles from him. I even started to resent it a little. I almost usta think he cared more about those pickles and my friends more than he cared about us." I paused a bit. "Then, one day I realized, 'Those pickles ain't for free!' Everybody usta say Dad had the greatest pickles in the world an' he just *gives 'em away!'*"

"Those pickles were just one a his tricks that put you through college, Al."

"The whole entire neighborhood usta come in an fill up on his corned beef and pastrami just so's they could get some of his extra 'free' pickles!"

"Dad was an entrepreneurial genius." My older brother's voice even reminded me of Dad. Except for that raspiness. That never showed signs of being there back in our past.

"We are going to Henri *aujourd'hui?*" spoke Marie.

"*Oui.*"

"I will see him *avec* Allan. *Tu et Jean figurez an programme pour les* screenings *aujourd'hui avec Robert et Jacques Benet. N'est ce pas?*"

"Oui. Oui."

"How are they—What do they have to do with any of this?"

"Jean Tourneaux, *le producters.* The producer. He's been supporting our causes for many years. His money has backed us in many operations. His production company has provided several of our operations and operators with solid legitimate covers.

"Jacques, our director and my co-star, Robert, they are not involved, Alain. They know nothing of our activities."

"Why do you want me to go with you to Henri, Paully?" I suddenly felt that cold hard knot travelling up to my throat.

"Henri is a dangerous man, Allan. He is very paranoid."

"He already threatened my life if I went back to New York before he . . . uh—you . . . uh—before whatever it is he thinks you are planning to do this week is done."

"I know. I spoke to him yesterday. Right after *our* telephone chat." There was that wry twisting grin again. "I told him we'd both be stopping by this afternoon on his boat. You just play along with me. Everything is going to be fine."

"Oh yeah?"

TWELVE

On the road to Cannes, Paully filled me in on some more of his missing twenty years. It seemed he did not work for the French equivalent of the CIA either. He was more of a free lancer—heading up a collection of other idealists more loyal to ideas than to individual nations and/or geopolitical boundaries. Their main idea was an ideal system of capitalism. While in Vietnam, Paul not only saw we, as a nation, had no genuine threat to our geological borders, he also came to see socialism—communism—had no place. No real future in the world. North Vietnam was a very bleak place. Cold. Drab. People walking with their heads down, dispirited. The only real solution, they thought, was a cleaned up version of capitalism. World Capitalism. Capitalism with a conscience. Communism was a world without a soul. It was doomed to failure.

So would capitalism be doomed too if not kept in check. Greed could rob the heart just as thoroughly as bureaucracy and living for the State could dissipate the soul.

"We work with the CIA when they need us—and we agree with them. They are, after all, on the side of capitalism. When they are too avaricious we *don't* work too well with them."

"The president is really gonna let you back in, Paully?"

"Charlie Shrubman is a reasonable man. They outlasted the Iran-Contra scandal before you say you voted for him." Paul looked at me sideways as he drove along the Riviera drive. "He is aware of how long it's been since Vietnam. And how sick the American public is of political scandal. Besides. Just in case he doesn't—that's why I sent for you here."

"I could always expand my accounting firm to Europe."

"You are daydreaming. No you can't. You know nothing of the various tax laws and regulations."

He was right. Besides, I'd spent the last twelve or thirteen years tirelessly building up my accounting firm to where we were now fast becoming one of the more prestigious firms in New York. We were not Price Waterhouse yet. But I could not entrust its day to day operations to any of my associates just so I could operate independently on the European continent. At least, not at this point anyway.

"What do you want me to do with Henri?"

"He needs a new money launderer. One a his usual banks is about to be investigated. He doesn't know why I really sent for you. I told him I wanted to try to bring you in as a person who could hide our financial activities for us. He knows how I can't go back home again. And how much I always talk about you."

Tears welled up inside me.

"You know how to launder his money on this deal for him—and for us. You know some safe 'investments' for him. That's all."

"Sounds easy enough," I said feeling that cold hard knot in my throat dissolve, taking some of that numbness in my body and head away with it.

THIRTEEN

Paul pulled off the Promenade de la Croisette in Cannes and parked his Peugeot on a side street a half a block from the beach. We stepped out of his yellow convertible, turned toward the sun drenched *Gulf de Napoule* and trudged through the clean white sand to the shoreline.

"Put your eyeballs back in their sockets, Al."

I looked at him with hoisted eyebrows and a smirk on my face.

"What's a matter?" he said. "Ya never seen semi-nude bathing beauties before in your life?"

"Not so many all at once. Or so semi-naked."

"What a sheltered life you must be leading."

How right he was, I just realized.

Just then I saw an unpleasant sight on the beach. Enough to put my eyes back a little.

"Henri," my brother extended. "You are looking robust."

The slob smiled, exposing his filthy uneven teeth. *"Mais, oui."* Closely matching mustard stains adorned his white tank top shirt. "I see you *did* bring along junior." I could smell stale wine evaporating through his wide spaced discolored teeth.

"Shall we go out to your ship?"

"Come. Step into the rowboat. *Alors.*"

I boarded his dinghy first, ahead of my brother so as not to be able to smell him too much.

When we got out to his yacht I was very impressed. Not because I did not think an international gun runner could not afford such a large boat. But because, how could such a grotesque human being as this have such impeccable taste? I could not figure this person.

"You like my ship, *petite frere?*"

"It's really you!"

"Your *frere, Monsieur* Capstein. I keep seeing more and more of you in him."

He looked me up and down. Then gave me a pat on the back.

"Alle. We will go below for—How you say?—cocktails?"

Henri Beauchamps led the way down the beige carpeted runway into a rather large—shockingly—beautifully decorated living/conference room type area. Picassos lined the stained oak panelled walls.

Stuffed rich dark chocolate leather upholstered chairs and a sofa beckoned weary travellers, vacationers, or entrepreneurs alike.

"*Tu* prefer scotch, as your brother?"

"Fine. Fine."

What a class act he was putting on. He poured us two drinks; then sat down behind a large carved oak desk in the far corner—to keep his waiting, uncorked bottle of port from crying—being too lonely without him so long atop his desk.

"So. You have already met my brother, Henri."

"You are not being *de bonne foi avec moi, Monsieur* Capstein. You were supposed to send *pour ton frere, l' accountant* next month. *Apres le festival de la cinema.*"

"Pardon, Henri. *Mais tu connaies*—you know I cannot tell you everything. *Les Iraqis* suspect Washington is on to them. As I told you *sur le telephone, ils pensent s'il ne devenent pas les leurs*—," my brother looked at me. "If they can't get their missing detonators by the beginning of the summer *les Americains* can mobilize their troops in enough time to thwart their efforts."

"*Alors.* We must move *rapidement. Ton frere, il comprendre quel son role doit etre, je l'espere.* He did not seem so eh, knowledgeable *l'autre soir a moi.*"

"We spoke, my brother *et moi* since then. He knows just what to do for you, Henri. You needn't worry too much." I looked at Henri and my brother poker-faced as Paully took a casual sip on his scotch. "I heard all the details of your untimely paid visit on them *l'autre soir.*" There was Paully's twisting sense of humor again. "You should know by now we'd never betray you, Henri."

"You left me *dans le noir.*" He took a swig of port from the mouth of his sweating companion—his bottle—staring directly into Paul's eyes.

"You are still our envoy to Hussein. You already committed enough cash up front to finance the deal. Don't keep flipping out on us *ici.* It's too big to screw up."

"*Pardon moi, Monsieur Capstein. Mais tu pouves le comprendre l'inquietude.*"

"Not only are you gonna get to keep your share of the pot. But, *apres mon frere,* Allan here gets to work, you'll *never* have to worry about anybody being able to trace down your new oil fields. *Et*—how you say?— liquid assets."

Paul's smile lit up the room as he winked at me. I, in turn, raised my glass toward *Monsieur* Beauchamps and nodded.

"My brother knows how to do the laundry. He will have your assets starched and shining."

Henri looked at me, his red eyes squinting. "You do look so *right* for this."

"Trust me, Henri. I'll have you all looking like a British tea drinking society."

"Hey. I do like *ton petite frere, Monsieur* Capstein. He's got lots of—how you say?—maxie."

"Moxie."

"Yeah. Moxie. Class." He looked at me and raised his almost finished bottle of port. *"A vous, Monsieur Capstein. Salut."*

"Salut." I raised my glass in response and took a swallow, wondering what this gentleman knew about class.

The rest of the meeting proceeded smoothly. Henri polished off his wine knowing he was to meet with Hussein as soon as he could set a meeting up.

"You contact the leaders. Tell them we have the merchandise. You know the terms we can accept."

"Oui, Monsieur Capstein. Leave it to me." Leave it to Beaver, I thought. "We don't get enough of his oil— he does not get what we have for him. *N'est ce pas?"* Henri displayed his yellow unevenly spaced teeth again for us.

"Voila." Paully looked at me. "Where is your Papa, Henri?"

"Il est dans Brussels. Something to do with the Soviet's problem."

"The Soviet's problem?" I asked.

"Nothing to do with us here, *petite frere.* They have no food on their shelves. Soon they either have civil war or the West helps them out of it."

"You are keeping things shipshape for him *ici?*" Paully inquired of him.

"*Ad bien sur, Monsieur Capstein!*"

"*Bien. Alors.* I guess my brother and I can go back ashore *maintenant,*" Paully asserted as he got up.

"*Mais oui,*" our gracious host responded. And he staggered up to escort us back to his dinghy and attempt to row us back to the beach.

"Let me know immediately when you have things set up with these 'gentlemen'."

Henri appreciated the touch of sarcasm in my brother's razor-edged voice.

"*Ad bien sur, Monsieur Capstein.*"

Then he turned to me as we were all standing.

"*Je suis desole*—I am sorry *pour* how we had to meet that first evening, *Monsieur* Capstein."

"Don't worry about it. You have a lot at stake."

"*Ton frere. Il est un bon homme.*"

Henri gave me another slap across the shoulders as we walked up the runway and crossed the deck to board his ship-to-shore transport. I thought I noticed a strange kind of fear twitching in his bloodshot eyes when he looked at me. Suddenly, I felt his paranoia and mistrust radiate onto my shoulders.

Once finally ashore and away from the crowded beach, Paully and I started talking about our bizarre business meeting.

"So. How do you like international business and politics, Allan?"

"I'm responding much better than I ever thought I would at this point."

"You were always a much better man than I noticed you ever gave yourself credit for, growing up."

"What a ya mean?"

"I don't know.—You remember that little retarded girl, lived down the other enda the block? All the kids around your age used to pick on her all the time?"

"Yeah. Why?"

"You were the only one usta stand up for her."

"She was a nice girl."

"Yeah. All the other kids usta tease you for it. They usta say *you* were retarded."

"Yeah. Till the time I flattened Freddie Glickerman for it." I stared across the *Promenade de la Croisette* picturing Freddie lying there, blood coming out the corner of his mouth.

"That's just what I'm talkin' about, Al. Freddie was bigger than you."

"He was a big, fat bully. He had it coming to him."

"And *you* gave it to him. Everybody else was scared to death a the kid, but you."

"Who said I wasn't scared of him? I just had enough of his bull. That's all." I then shifted my thoughts back to today. "How come Beauchamps has such a classy-looking yacht?"

"He can afford it. Besides," smiled my brother, "it belongs to his father."

"Uh huh. You wanna tell me how come he was so overanxious about me knowing how to launder his assets?"

"You tell me."

"Did you plant any subliminal messages on my computer about that too?"

"No. But *Monsieur* Henri Beauchamps thinks we did."

"Oh."

FOURTEEN

We walked along the boulevard to Tourneaux's hotel in order to meet Marie. We had to start pushing through a crowd of cameras and reporters on the plaza only to hear a voice from the center of attention call.

"Alain! *Ici. Ici!*"

All the spectators and reporters turned around to see who the voice was beckoning to, and the video cameras swung around and were now facing me and Paul. I self-consciously walked up to the center of attention and Marie kissed me. I could feel the crowd's clamor.

"*Ou est votre ami, Mlle. Du Berge?*" asked an eager young interviewer pointing his microphone at her mouth.

"*C'est Alain Capstein. Allan est mon bon ami a New York.*"

The interviewer asked me something in French too quickly for me to begin to understand.

"Je parle surtout English."

"Ah. Pardon moi. Do you ah—Are you knowing Mlle. Du Berge for too long?"

"Yes. For too long." I smiled at her.

"You are also *dans le cinema?"*

"No. No. *Je suis* an accountant."

"An accountant?—*Ah, oui."*

The interviewer then turned from me toward Marie and continued in his native language. Marie kept radiating warmth and vitality, giggling and squeezing my arm from time to time. Soon, she took my hand and led us away waving behind her as she headed us to the gambling casino. Another young actress, it appeared, had newly captured the attention of the interviewers and reporters and their marauding camera crews.

"That guy does not think too much of accountants, does he?"

"He wanted to know if we are to marry."

"What did you say?"

"Rien pas. Nothing. Keep them guessing. Then they want to come back for more."

"You are so innocent looking."

"Je suis." Her wild blue-green eyes did not, as usual, betray any facade. No wonder she was nominated for Outstanding Actress of the Year.

We walked into the casino and gravitated to the roulette wheel. I bought some chips with my own money, Paul bought some of his own, and Marie stayed with me as Paully wandered off to the black-jack table.

The atmosphere in the room was electric. Even though I live two hours north of Atlantic City, New Jersey, this was the first time I'd ever been inside a gambling casino. It was not the same as the stock market. There, your wagers are much more educated guesses than here. Here, it's all a roll of the dice, or a spin of the wheel. In the same space of time it would have taken me to drive down to Atlantic City from home, I'd made a fortune, lost a fortune and begun to almost break even. Though it approximated the Stock Exchange, it was a lot quicker and a lot less cerebral. That evening was to be a similar one for the filmmakers. It was awards night for the stars.

Marie's cast and crew were up for six awards including best picture, best director and best actor and actress. Few pictures ever capture more than one or two trophies at Cannes, I was told. They try to be very diplomatic.

Nonetheless, the tension and fever could be felt building throughout the daylight hours. After a light dinner in the *Chateau de Lerins* restaurant back atop *Mont Chevalier*, Marie had a chauffeur driven limousine, provided by her film studio, take us to the awards ceremony. I was to be Mlle. Du Berge's escort for the evening.

That hard knot of fear was coming back inside of me. Only, this time it was not that hard. Nor was it cold. It was warm. And pulsating. And joyous. I felt as if I had died and gone to heaven.

Paul went back to Paris instead of joining us for the occasion. He had lots of business to catch up on, he told us. And to spend some time with that girlfriend of his he alluded to the night we reunited.

I recognized a few of the American film people in the auditorium. Spike Lee was sitting to the left and behind us. Jessica Lange and Jack Nicolson were nearby as well.

Flashbulbs were crackling like popcorn. Cameras were scanning the throngs. Spotlights endlessly criss-crossed the crowd. Outside, as each limo drove to the entrance an announcer told the spectators who was stepping out to rush inside past them. Not bad for an accountant from Manhattan I thought, as I stepped out and escorted Marie by her right arm.

"Marie Du Berge et—et t'ami Monsieur Alain Capstein, d'Amerique!" barked the announcer through the loud-speaker to her fans.

This *is* a fantasyland, I thought. I was floating on air as we breezed inside amidst the tension and rhythms of excitement and expectations.

I half-expected to see Eddie Murphy or Billy Crystal emceeing the ceremonies. I was half-correct. A

French comedian shortly took center stage and broke into a Jerry Lewis impression to start things off.

Sitting to the left and right of Marie and myself were the same people we had dinner with that first night in France. Minus Lucille—Tourneaux's cook and servant. They only temporarily reminded me of that package that brought me here and all else that had happened in such a short period of time.

So much was happening. And so much more seemed certain to take place in the next few days. These awards almost seemed trivial compared to the war—with possible usage of nuclear weapons—that may soon be erupting in the Middle East. I looked around the hall. Everyone smiling. In their tuxedos. And three thousand dollar gowns. Expectant. Hopeful. Exuberant. Paully was attempting to head off World War III at this very moment. Spectacular. What were the Iraqi soldiers thinking right now, marching toward destruction? I wondered.

Most of the minor awards were handed out first. Best Costume Design. Best Makeup. Best Animation of a Short Subject. Etcetera, etcetera . . .

The suspense kept building. Who was going to win the coveted *Palm D'Or?* The international award for Best Picture of the Year? Who, indeed was going to be chosen Best Actor or Best Actress?

Jean Tourneaux looked eloquent in his white tuxedo and red bow tie. No sign of worry on his face at all. Anticipation perhaps. He *was* the producer of the film. Jacques Benet was still scrutinizing the crowd. Give him a brush and canvas, I thought, and he'd slap together a masterpiece. No wonder he keeps winning awards for his art.

The nearer they got to announcing Best Actress of the Year, the more sweaty my palms got. So far, "our picture" won one award. Best cinematography. Best Actor went to Al Pacino.

It was now time for Best Actress. Marie's eyes lit up the spotlight that was beamed on her when her name was announced as the third nominee. Light danced in a thousand different directions off her blue-green sequin dress. A thirty second clip of film flashed across the silver screen filling the stage with her work. Then, applause. Next, the two remaining nominees had their spotlights and thirty second moments. Then, applause. It was now time . . .

"And the winner for Best Actress in a Motion Picture is . . . Anne Parillaud!"

I looked at Marie to console her. She was exuberant. Applauding for Ms. Parillaud. That was when I thought I felt myself falling in love with her.

The rest of the night went without a hitch. Except maybe for Spike Lee storming out when his movie, *Do the Right Thing* did not win the *Palm D'Or.* Jean Tourneaux did not storm out when the award went to someone else's movie as well. Perhaps he had other thoughts on his poker-faced mind. Hussein had to be taken out.

FIFTEEN

Things started moving even quicker. CNN news reported an alarming buildup of troops along the Southern Iraqi border. According to the CNN report the next morning on French TV, thirty thousand more troops were marching toward the Kuwaiti border to reinforce the troops that were already standing there. I started to get that cold hard knot in my stomach as I watched.

"President Hussein has assured the world that he is not preparing to attack the tiny oil-rich kingdom of Kuwait. Whatever it is he might be doing along the Kuwaiti border is not clear at this time."

"Sure," I uttered from Marie's sofa.

"Do not worry so much Alain. *Ton frere.* He will know what to do."

"You trust Henri to be able to set it up right? He doesn't even know he's being used for anything." I placed my hand on my abdomen.

"*Monsieur* Capstein. He will know how to do it. Do not worry so much."

My head started spinning again. I did not want to lose my brother Paully so shortly after I found him alive again after so many years.

"When I was growing up in New York I used to play shortstop. That's a certain position in baseball. Paul was on the high school and college varsity team. I used to think he'd be a professional baseball player some day."

Marie looked at me and came closer.

"Your brother told me of you. He told me how tough you always were. He said, when you were growing up, you did not talk too much. But when you did, it was usually to stand up for something. Or somebody."

"He told you that?"

"*Mais oui*, Alain." Marie came even closer, still in her nightie. "You turned out even better than he described how you were, growing up, to be."

She put her hands on my shoulders. I pulled her to me.

"I think I am falling in love with you, Mlle. Du Berge." I kissed her neck and cheek near her left ear.

"*Je pense*—I think I am falling in love with you too."

That afternoon around two o'clock the telephone rang. Marie picked it up, then handed me the receiver. It was Paully.

"I'll see you this evening at Jean's hotel."

"What's going on?"

"You will know then. Meet us in Tourneaux's room. *A* six *heurs.*"

"Six o'clock?"

"*Oui.* Six o'clock."

The line went dead. I should have been more scared, I thought. But I was not.

"We have to go to Jean's room tonight. At six."

"OK," replied my French lover. "*Alors.* We shall go swimming out in the sea. *N'est ce pas?*"

"*Mais oui,*" I obliged.

Sixteen

As the door to number 614 opened at six P.M., my heart sped up. Seated in a plush armchair was Paul wearing a white short sleeve shirt and white linen pants. Next to him stood a pretty Asian woman about my age.

"Come in, Alain," begged Jean Tourneaux holding the door for Marie and myself. *"Allo,* Marie."

They kissed each other on each cheek.

"Hello, *Monsieur* Tourneaux." I shook his extended hand.

"Allan." My brother put his drink down and stood up. "This is my good friend, Poon Li." They looked at each other humorously.

"Hello."

"Poon Li is the woman I've been mentioning to you."

"Mentioning?" she scolded. "How do you do?" She walked forward and kissed me on each cheek. "Your brother talks of you to me frequently."

"Thanks." I looked at Paully.

"What will you have to drink?" asked Jean.

"Soulement, mais un coke-a-cola pour moi, Jean."

"And a scotch and soda for you, Alain?"

"How did you know?"

"A lucky guess. I thought it might run in your *famille.*"

"Oui. Oui. That it does." I cast a glance at Paully who was sipping from his amber-filled glass.

Marie sat on the sofa and I quickly sat beside her.

"So. How long have you two been together?" I asked.

"They have known each other forever," replied my girlfriend immediately.

"We first met in 1979. During the Khmer Rouge holocaust. There was too much pressure on us not to do anything about what was going on there. I met Poon Li just after they ransacked and burned her village. We both got out of there. A couple a years later we met again in Paris."

"Your brother is very modest. I wanted somehow to make a film about what happened in my country. I thought I would ask Monsieur Tourneaux—Jean—if he would be interested. After talking to him he realized it must have been your brother who took me and saved my life. So he brought us together again. And, we are still together."

"*Voila*," I replied, wanting my drink.

"*Ici*, Alain. Marie." Jean handed us our drinks just at the right moment. I thanked him and took a long sip.

"I see you and Marie are doing all right together."

"Yeah. We're OK." I placed my hand on her thigh and gave her a firm yet gentle squeeze.

"*N'est ce pas?*" she responded.

"Henri made contact with the maniac last night, Al. He's setting things up in Baghdad."

"Baghdad? Isn't that too dangerous?"

"Maybe not. I told him, 'If you can't get him out to Paris or somewhere else—insist on making the deal in the airport.'"

"How'r ya gonna do it?"

"Friday. That's when we're all gonna meet them."

"All? What do you mean, *all?*"

"You are going to go with Beauchamps. You're the laundry man. You are going to set up all the hidden paperwork."

"Wait a minute, Paully. I can't do all a that."

"Sure you can. Just ask Henri. *He knows you can.*"

I still felt calmer than expected.

"I'm still workin' out the details. Tomorrow, you give Beauchamps the detonating device you brought over from New York."

"*What?*" I stiffened in my seat.

"It's a dummy. It won't work even if he *does* get his hands on it."

"You let me travel with that *thing* in my hands?"

"That was what Henri was really looking for that evening. He thought—"

"How can you leave me sitting there with a nuclear detonating device in my lap? What if I got caught with it?"

"You had an armed escort. Remember?"

"Yeah. But—"

"How hard was it to go through customs, Al?"

"I don't know. They didn't ask me too much. But—"

I looked around the room at everyone. Paul had that twinkle in his eyes.

"So. They knew what I was carrying. Huh, Paul?"

"Would *I* let you get arrested?"

"Shit!"

Jean looked at me, amused.

"I'm not too used to this kind a stuff, Paully."

"You look cool enough."

"Oh yeah?" I bit off and swallowed a gulp of air; then let it out slowly through clenched teeth.

"Tomorrow, you give Henri the device. Then—let him tell you how he set up the entire meeting. You can handle it."

"Fuck your sense of humor, Paully." Marie laughed and grabbed my arm. "So this guy is almost like a father to you, huh?" I looked at her, but could not help smiling back.

"Would you like another drink, Alain?" Jean Tourneaux assessed my demeanor with neutral eyes.

"No. This one was good enough."

"You are doing fine, Alain."

"Sure." I retorted. I looked around the room and let out a deep breath. I looked through the doorway into the bedroom and thought I noticed a small alarm clock on Tourneaux's night table next to his bed. "Anybody eat any supper yet around here? I think I'm a little hungry."

"I'll call room service." Jean suddenly seemed to have more color in his face. "What shall we order?"

"Filet mignon?" I asked.

SEVENTEEN

Like clockwork, Henri Beauchamps showed up at Marie's home the following morning promptly at ten A.M. At least, he was punctual. He drove up in a huge black Mercedes Benz and parked it half in the driveway, half on the grass.

"He's wearing a clean shirt," I remarked to my sweetheart.

"*Allo.* Alain!" He managed a weak leering smile as he slammed the door to his automobile shut. I shuddered inside as I saw his outstretched arms coming toward me. "*You* are in good spirits." He shot a perverted look at Marie next to me upon greeting me with that remark.

"Hello Henri. You look in good spirits yourself this morning," I answered.

"Ah. *Oui.*" He grabbed my right hand and gave it a bone crushing squeeze.

"*You* are looking in good spirits too, *mon Cherie.*" He let go the grip on my hand to leer at her some more.

"Give up, Henri."

I felt like throwing up. But I asked him to come in anyway.

"*Apres tu.*" What charm he could muster when he wanted to.

We talked for at least another hour; Henri trying to impress me on how he helped finance and/or supply other regional conflicts in the past. He even told me how he got a piece of the Iran-Contra arms action for himself.

"It was easy. Your *Americain* Congress made me quite a *paquet.* As soon as they made it illegal to supply the Contras, I knew I would have a fresh market. With some old partners. I give your Colonel Oliver North all the credit. The CIA never had a better salesperson than the Colonel. He helped speed up Gorbechev's Glastnost, as well, you know."

"How?" I was revolted.

"How, do you ask?" Henri's laugh did nothing to soothe my nausea. "The Ruskies, they cannot afford to prop up all their puppets around the globe anymore. They cannot adequately feed their people. How can they afford to support a foreign war anymore to spread their failing ideology?"

I could not argue with him there. Henri was crass. Tasteless. But he was not that stupid. I could see something more in him than I thought was there up until that moment.

"How're ya gonna handle the meeting with Hussein Friday?"

"Ou est l'engin?"

"What?"

"Where is the device?"

"I will bring it," Marie announced.

She quickly jumped up and bounced into her bedroom after it.

"Why could I not find it *l'autre soir?"*

"You did not look hard enough!"

I knew why. Marie showed me a little trick in her bedroom closet last night. Turn the right hook on the inside wall counterclockwise one complete revolution—And, *voila!* The rear panel behind the first shelf over her clothes rack will slide open exposing a multi-purpose storage compartment. The device was safely tucked away inside that compartment that evening by the time Henri showed up.

Marie swept the device off the top of her dresser where she'd placed it after she awoke in the morning; then came back and presented it to Mr. Beauchamps.

"Voila!" His burning-red eyes glowed coldly. He examined it closely. *"Ainsi. C'est la cle."*

He looked it over like the proud papa of an illegitimate newborn child. Such tenderness. Such care. Such malevolence in his stare.

"We will keep this *ici*," he finally replied. "Until we go to the airport tomorrow."

"Tomorrow is Wednesday. I thought we'd be going Friday morning."

"*Non*, my good friend. We are to stay at the Royal Palace overnight. Then celebrate the deal Thursday."

"But—I thought we were to meet Hussein at the airport." I felt that cold hard knot in my stomach reappear.

"Naw. He insisted we come to the palace." His cold smoldering eyes looked at me. "Do not worry so much. We are his friends. Why do you look nervous?"

"I—I thought my brother told you to set things up at the airport."

"Sometimes *ton frere, Monsieur* Capstein, *he* worries too much. *That* is where you get it from, *petit frere*. Do not worry. Saddam is a good man. I've done business with him before."

"Yeah. I guess."

"You just tell him how you will arrange the ah, financial paperwork. Leave the rest to me. He will like you."

The rest of our rendezvous went smoothly enough. Saddam was to send an army contingent to greet us at Baghdad International Airport. We would be taken directly to his palace, shown our accommodations and have dinner with the president.

The next day would be for business. If things went according to plan, as my compatriot assured me they would, that newborn baby still in Henri's arms would be flown by my brother the following noon into Baghdad.

"Paully is gonna fly it in himself, huh?"

"Why do you worry so much, *Monsieur accountant?*" I took no offence to him as I did during our first brief encounter. "*Ton frere* can fly an airplane." Henri showed me his uneven yellow teeth. As usual, he needed a shave.

"I guess we will fly out before my brother gets there."

"*Pourquoi?* Saddam will most likely provide us with some good entertainment after the arrangements are assured."

"Yes. I am sure."

"Do not enjoy yourself too much, Alain," pouted Marie.

"Ah. Love. It is such a foolish emotion. But, you are too young still to know, *mon cherie.*"

I just realized how pale Henri's face was under his whiskers for someone who spent so much time along the French Riviera.

"*Et tu.* You are too wise to know different."

"One day, *mon cherie.* Then you will see."

"You sound like a man who has been wounded by love."

"Love. War. It is both all the same. *N'est ce pas?* You must take all that you can *mon ami.* You must take what you can."

"Yeah." I looked Henri Beauchamps up and down. Was he always such a monster? Why did I want to know? I wondered.

We engaged in a little more small talk. I learned through Henri that his father and Marie's old man worked together in Vietnam long before the French regime had failed. Henri helped himself to his usual bottle of wine and found some sharp cheddar cheese to go with it deep in Marie's refrigerator. Between gulps and bites, with crumbs clinging to his lips and whiskers near his mouth, he continued telling us how he realized loyalties to self far superseded any "self-serving" states or nationalities.

"As long as you do not antagonize—or embarrass—especially embarrass any government or official too greatly you owe nothing to anybody but to yourself. *Mon pere,* he stayed in Indo-China far after the French left." Henri seemed to refer to his own French government as something foreign. "He made his money by keeping a low profile. No embarrassments. No problems.

"Armaments are a great commodity. Keep a low profile. Keep the warriors happy." He laughed vaguely, absently moistening and yellowing his sleeve, wiping it against his mouth. "Soon—the governments—they come to you. The Superpowers. Ha, ha. The *Super*powers—They let you know who they think should have more or less. Or this or that. It is a funny game."

I let him talk, wondering which superpowers would ever be letting him sell Saddam Hussein a nuclear detonator.

"You do not look too amused." His crimsoned eyes glistened insanely at me.

"Who knows you are planning to sell that thing to the Iraqis?

"You do, *mon ami. Tu et moi.* And a select few others you have recently met."

"No other superpowers?"

"Ah. You are missing the point. Keep a low profile. Who cares about a small dictator in the middle of a desert?" He wiped some more yellow crumbs and red stains onto his jacket sleeve. "Keep a strong balance. One side versus the other. Everyone is happy. *N'est ce pas?*"

"Who else has nuclear weapons against him?"

"You Jews do."

"*What?*"

"The Israelis."

"Mmmph. Yeah. The Israelis. That is the truth." I also knew that Israel was not on Hussein's borders.

Nor were any of his troops marching toward *their* borders. The Kingdom of Kuwait was hardly in the direction of the State of Israel. I decided not to discuss this minor point with Henri. Why mix logic with profits?

"Smile *Monsieur Accountant*. By this weekend you will be a very rich man." Henri raised the bottle of burgundy to his lips only missing a few drops down his chin.

As soon as Monsieur Henri Beauchamps got through telling me where and when to meet him at the airport the next day; then took his, now more appropriately for him, dirty shirt and jacket on his back out the front door and into his black Mercedes Benz with him and took off, I asked Marie if I could use her telephone.

I still had an accounting firm to maintain in New York and had to make some important telephone calls to some of my clients and my associates back home. New York was, at that point, another planet. No nuclear weapons. None *I* was aware of. No arms deals. At least none on this major a scale. Just stocks, bonds and assorted real estate, etcetera.

"Do you not think you should wait until it is daylight in the States?" she responded when I told her my purposes.

"I forgot. You're right." I held my right hand out in front of me. It was not shaking.

"*Bientot*. Soon it will be all over, Alain. Soon."

"You wanna come back to New York with me next week?"

"*Mais oui!*"

"*Voila!*"

EIGHTEEN

Paully came back to Antibes that afternoon with Poon Li and another man, in his fifties, I thought. We greeted them all. Paully introduced me to the gentleman with him and his girlfriend.

"Say hello to Viktor, Allan."

Although he was frail-looking—tall and bony, with slicked back steel-grey hair pushed slightly forward producing a pompadour—he had a very firm hand-shake.

"Hello, Mr. Allan Capstein," he greeted.

Viktor had a familiar sounding accent. I'd heard it in New York a lot. Though in New York you will hear almost any kind of accent in existence, this particular accent was becoming more and more prevalent on the streets.

"You sound Russian," I replied.

"You have a very good ear." He laughed heartily.

"Viktor is a very good friend of ours, Al. He will be goin' along with me on our adventure."

I instinctively looked up and down the street.

"Why don't we all go inside."

I soon learned Viktor was a former KGB agent now doing a lot of free lance work around the globe. Among other things, he was an excellent marksman, I was told.

"One a his students probably shot me down," joked my brother, now sitting on the sofa.

What a totally incongruent pair, I thought. How could these two people be sitting in the same room together? I slowly started to comprehend.

"Viktor defected from the Soviet Union ten years ago when Leonid Brezhnev was still in power."

"Yes. I did not like spying for a false ideology. The more I was with KGB the more I realized communism was finished. Sure, the West has its problems. Crime is a major part of its culture. But under communism, the people cannot have too much. In way of possessions they are lucky to have a TV. Let alone good food on the table. In spirit they have no reason for much hope for better. Everything is for the State. Not much room for the individual. No. I could not defend that system any longer. Gorbechev is our only hope."

"You still consider yourself Russian?"

"I will always be Russian. I am no longer social-ist."

"How did you and my—Paully—ever get to-gether?" I wondered.

"This is long story," Viktor answered.

He explained how when he first defected, he needed a place to hide for a while. Until his former colleagues would get tired of looking for him. Or not be afraid of what he might say of them any longer. He contacted the one woman who he felt might be the most receptive to him right away without having to seek political asylum in the United States. The wife of a man he had done some business with while still in Vietnam. Mme. Du Berge. Marie's mother.

"Battle lines are not always so clearly defined. Are they, Al?" asked Paul.

"I suspected even in Vietnam, perhaps, commu-nism was not the way. *Monsieur* Du Berge. He began to open my eyes. Even though we knew the West could never win there, *he* was winning. He had something that *was* working. Entrepreneurship. He made sense to me."

"Why did you think Mme. Du Berge would take you in?"

"I was with *Monsieur* Du Berge the day he died." I felt Marie stiffen. "It is about time you knew the truth, my darling." Marie's eyes widened, turning a deeper shade of green.

"Your father's car went off the side of the road into a ravine after the left rear tire was shot out from underneath him. He was trying to stop his young entrepreneurs from dealing with drugs."

"Who killed him?" Marie demanded.

"My superior officer was skimming profits from all the growers and dealers. He did not like your father talking them out of the drug business. It hurt his share of profits. I am sorry. I wish I did not have to tell you, Marie."

"I knew it was no accident, Viktor."

"I was working with *Monsieur* Du Berge to talk them out of the drug business myself. We knew most of drugs went to U.S. But I never liked it. Some of our people were getting some too. It destroys people."

I thought I understood Viktor Durzinsky well enough. He was an honest capitalist, ex-socialist still loyal to his Motherland, Russia.

"I knew your father talked of me to your mother. So when it was time to go, I knew I would try to contact her."

"She never told me how Papa was killed."

"She is a mother. She will always try to protect you," Viktor answered.

I took Marie's hand in mine. She smiled weakly at me.

"When did you meet my brother?"

"Not long afterwards. We knew who he was. Back in 1973 we thought he might be a converted communist. We knew CIA was after him. Some of our agents tried to recruit him. We traced him to France in mid-seventies."

"Yeah," interjected my brother at last. "They thought, if I was hiding from the CIA, I'd be able to be bought. They were funny."

"What a ya mean?"

"Just 'cause your government does a few things you don't like or don't approve of; doesn't mean you're gonna wanna turn on it or overthrow 'em or anything."

"Another reason I think communism is finished. They are too rigid. Too scared of dissent. They are collapsing under their own weight."

"What a ya think they'll do if the U.S. has to send in troops against this Hussein character?"

"At this point? Nothing. God protect Gorbechev. He will open up everything for the people."

Viktor Durzinsky was an eye opener. The last five days were an eye opener. It was mesmerizing. My head stopped spinning a while ago. Only because I got used to it spinning around in its skull, I think. I could not tell if it was turning around and around in its encasement or not any longer at that point. Reality gave way to Hades; his realm became reality. Then it soon did not feel that much like hell any longer. Viktor showed me there *was* some humanity behind the so-called Iron Curtain. Boundaries were melting in the haze. A new order had to take its place for me.

"Allan. We will fly to Baghdad after you let us know it's all right. Saddam is a crazy man. He probably won't let you leave until he is holding his merchandise in his hands. Enjoy his hospitality." Paul shot a glance at Marie. "If you can. We'll handle the rest. Me an' Viktor."

"How? What are ya gonna do?"

"Detonators blow things up. Don't they?"

"I was demolitions expert in KGB. We will detonate the madman."

Twenty years ago the troops Viktor might have personally trained himself almost killed my brother. Today, both men, knowingly, sat in the same room together plotting the assassination of a Middle Eastern megalomaniac. My head must still have been spinning.

NINETEEN

We spent the rest of the afternoon getting acquainted and reacquainted. Poon Li disappeared into the kitchen with Marie, soon to prove herself to be one of the great cooks of the Western—or, Eastern—world. I finally found the time to get in touch with some of my clients and associates back home and check on some much more mundane, but just as necessary for me, business. The world could soon be going to hell. But it still kept spinning. Business was going slowly for me back home. We were in a recession. Another good reason for a military diversion, I thought.

"Paully. What are ya gonna do back in the States after this is over?" I needed to be optimistic.

"If the president lets me back? I don't know. I may go back to school. I know how to blow things to pieces.

I may just learn how to put buildings together after all."

I still could not get over how much he resembled Dad.

"You may not wanna go back to visit the old neighborhood."

"Why not?"

"Things changed." That was an understatement. "Remember the movie theater?"

"Yeah. The Chester. Twenty-six cents for the kiddie matinee all day Saturday." I could see the twenty-five 'free' color cartoons playing deep in Paully's reminiscing brown eyes.

"It's gone. They tore it down years ago." The cartoons just stopped shining and went blank in his eyes. "They turned it into a . . . a flea market at first."

"They usta show x-rated movies there for a while."

"Yes. Just about the time you enlisted. That's when I began to notice things changing. The corner candy store? Became an off-track betting parlor."

"Yeah? That musta put the old shoe shine parlor across the street outta business."

"They did disappear right about the same time. Why? He was always doing a good business I always thought."

"He was the local bookie. Ever notice that blackboard with all his prices on it in front of his store every day?"

"Yeah. He sold all sorts a stuff in there. Hair-brushes. Shoe polish. Umbrellas."

"That blackboard opened up in the middle. Inside was all the odds from all the tracks that were running that day."

"You are kiddin' me!"

"No. I'm not kiddin you. Ever notice how he'd list, 'Umbrellas. Special today,' every so often?"

"I don't know."

"That meant there was a muddy track wherever there was a capitalized letter in the 'special' sign."

"No kiddin'."

"Large P meant Pimlico. Large Y was Yonkers. R stood for Roosevelt, A—Aqueduct."

"Whoa. No wonder his shoe shine parlor became a barber shop."

"No wonder." Paully's face was wistful. I thought I could see that blackboard opening up in his smile. "What became of that flea market? Where the Chester used to stand?"

"It's a . . . a vacant lot. Everyone moved out. Dad an Mom were lucky. They were one a the last to leave. Some schnook bought the deli. The neighborhood wasn't even so Jewish any more. The Blacks moved down from the Heights."

"How's the Italian restaurant. That still there?"

"Yeah. They'll never leave. They baked a huge cake for Mom an Dad when they finally left an went down to Florida."

"Yeah. I heard about that." I must have had a strange look on my face when he said that. "I told you I got people checkin' up on you, Allan."

"Paully?"

"Yeah?"

I took a long pause trying to express my feelings to him.

"Poon Li gonna come to the U.S. with you?"

"Poon Li. Yeah. She's gonna be comin' with us."

I looked toward the kitchen suddenly conscious of some clatter of pots and pans.

"Here. Take this."

Paully handed me a tissue. I didn't notice tears were dampening my eyes.

"Mom's gonna go nuts when she sees you, Paully." I absently dried my eyes.

"We'll handle that later."

Dinner gratefully came out of the kitchen on that chord. I looked across the room just in time to see Viktor's face changing from vague sobriety to one of relief. He slowly sat himself upright and leaned forward; then stood up clasping his hands hungrily in front of him.

"Ah. Let us enjoy Poon Li's fine Cambodian cooking." Viktor Durzinsky would *not* be going back home to *his* Motherland after our joint venture in Baghdad this weekend. I wondered if *his* parents were still alive or not. Or, if they were still alive, if they were aware of his present state of affairs.

The delicious aroma of South-East Asian cooking coming at us lifted us all to newer heights.

Reality was slowly sorting itself out.

Viktor, Poon Li and my brother stayed until nine o'clock that evening. I was not shocked to learn that Viktor was a master chess player. I tried my luck against him. I wound up amusing my new friend immensely. When it took him thirty-three minutes to defeat me the last time, I felt almost triumphant. Paul and Poon Li went out into the Mediterranean moonlight along the shore and took a long walk.

Marie decided to do some reading. I noticed she was learning her lines for her next screenplay as we were leaning over the chess board—Viktor and myself. I was growing more and more accustomed to my newfound life.

TWENTY

At nine-thirty the next morning the telephone rang. Marie handed the receiver to me after picking it up and answering it.

"*C'est Henri.*"

"All right," I sighed. "Let me have it.

"Hello, Henri."

"*Allo, mon ami.* Get dressed as a well-to-do businessman and meet me by the Lufthansa terminal at twelve noon. *N'est ce pas?*"

"*Aujourd'hui?*" I joked.

"*Aujourd'hui!* You are a comedian?"

"*Oui,*" I responded. "Twelve noon at Lufthansa. Dressed as a well-to-do businessman." I wondered how he would be dressed. As a well-to-do slob, I supposed.

"*Bien.* Be on time. I shall see you then."

"*Ah bientot.*" I hung up.

"Your French. It is getting better."

"Oui oui, mon cherie." I rolled over and resumed what we had been up to before Henri's phone call so rudely had interrupted us.

"Oui oui," she responded.

After breakfast, my sweetheart drove me into town where I still had a hardly used hotel room. I needed to pack an overnight bag. Enough for two days and a flight the hell out of Iraq.

She handed her keys to the valet who instantly recognized her. And we walked to the elevator and travelled to the second floor and then to my room down the hall.

I pointed to the "Do Not Disturb" sign I must have left hanging from the doorknob the first night, and we both got a big chuckle out of it.

I put my key into the keyhole and pushed open the door, then we walked in and were slapped in the face by the incredible mess. Clothes were everywhere. Drawers were ripped apart. Closet doors were open wide.

"Henri Beauchamps. He must have come *ici apres* he did not find *l' engin a ma maison* last Sunday."

"He must have come here the next day. After I took a few things to your place."

"Alors. We will pack quickly and leave."

When we pulled up to the Lufthansa terminal at the airport, I stepped out of Marie's red Porsche, took my suitcase and bade her good-bye.

She waved to me expectantly from her car.

"I'll be home soon," I said trying to smile, only semi-consciously aware of the fact that this French Riviera was not my home.

"I know," she bravely smiled in return.

I slowly turned and walked steadily into the terminal, then up to the departing gate and almost did not recognize the person in front of me. Dressed in an immaculately pressed charcoal pinstripe business suit, white starched shirt and almost matching striped tie—with outdated stick pin in its center—was a clean shaven, fresh smelling Henri Beauchamps.

"You are right on time, *mon ami,*" he greeted as I gawked at him.

"Nice clothes. *N'est pas?*" he gloated pulling on his shirt and jacket sleeves one at a time in front of his chest. I hardly noticed his stained teeth.

"Very impressive!"

We boarded the airplane, carrying our travel bags with us at Henri's insistence. The flight itself was uneventful. I could see no uniformed French soldiers on board this flight sitting anywhere near us. We obviously were winging it on our own.

As the airplane began its descent over the desert I started to think about my parents in the Florida heat. What would Dad make of this sand trap approaching the eighteenth green? *"Always use the right club when address-*

ing the ball. Line up your shot properly—and stroke the ball firmly." This was gonna be more of a rough shot than any straight line from the middle of any fairway, I thought.

The streamlined Lufthansa jet touched down in the oasis of Baghdad; and we grabbed our suitcases and disembarked. Waiting for us on the runway was our contingent of Iraqi soldiers. A handful of high ranking officers. I did not see their Commander-in-Chief—the president of this oil-laden sandbox amongst our welcoming committee.

"Allo, allo!" greeted Henri to his old friends.

"Salaam aleceim. Salaam aleceim," they all responded.

"This is my friend, Alain Capstein." Henri responded to wondering suspicious eyes. "He will be handling all the ah, legalities."

The Arab warriors looked at each other and grumbled in their native tongue. Then, finally, they turned to me.

"Salaam aleceim. Salaam aleceim, our friend Allan Capstein." I figured they had accepted the Jew as handshakes were traded all around. "You are not related to Mr. Paul Capstein, are you?"

"Paul is my brother."

"Mmm. A good man is your brother. Even for a Jewish man."

I loved their subtlety.

We were then taken to the palace where the president, we were told, was waiting for us. Along the route from Baghdad's Saddam International Airport—the president renamed it after himself—we got into small talk with our gracious hosts.

"You are never been to the Middle East before, Allan Capstein?"

"Uh, no sir, General Tazmin. I'm used to places with a little more water around me." At that, I noticed how the terrain appeared more muddy than sand-filled en route to the center of the capital of their nation.

"The desert. It makes a man of you. You are forced to rely on your own resources. You learn to survive."

The other officers laughed, affirming the sentiments of the general, as one of them opened the bar in the back of their stretch Lincoln and reached for a bottle of thick green liquid.

The lieutenant-colonel to my left poured a glass for me and my partner; then four more for himself and his partners. I noticed the road to the palace clumped with groups of soldiers; some on foot—others atop Soviet tanks.

"We will drink to the future. When peace for *all* Arabs will be secured!" the middle-aged lieutenant-colonel asserted.

I put my glass to my lips and took a shot. I shuttered upon swallowing and tried to catch my breath as I gasped out the tinted window.

"Is good. No, my friends!"

"Yeah," I gulped.

"Please. Some more," the rotund General Tazmin insisted, grabbing the clear glass bottle from the grasp of his cohort and lesser ranking senior officer. "Have another." I let him pour as Henri held his empty glass out eagerly in front of my glass for a refill.

"You will like our Baghdad, Mr. Capstein," spoke the officer with a thin leathery complexion and dusty moustache to my right. "Your friend, Mr. Beauchamps already knows our city well. He knows of its many charms."

"I told him he would love it here, Colonel. He will not be disappointed. *Je suis certainment.*" Henri leered at me as I ventured another shot of my green Schnapps.

I just witnessed another of those larger-than-life sized portraits of the president whiz by on the side of the road. That mosaic of Saddam dressing up his "Saddam International Airport" could be seen for miles as we descended and approached the landing strip.

A vague creepy darkness hung over the desert as we entered the city limits. A man in baggy pants gathered tightly at his ankles, ran out of an alley, diagonally across our path. He was clutching something close to his chest as he darted out. A loud commotion followed him swiftly. Suddenly, shots rang out and he fell on his face into an expanding pool of his own blood. A squawking sound came up from underneath him as a chicken nervously fluttered away from his lifeless body. One more shot rang out and the fowl fell still. Two soldiers walked past the man in the baggy pants amidst gently blowing feathers, picked up the dead bird and waved for some other soldiers to load the man's body onto the back of an old wood slatted pickup truck. Our chauffeur gave it a quick glance in his rearview mirror without slowing down an inch as we drove on by. Henri managed to raise his eyebrows and shoulders at me. Then he spoke to the Iraqi war-lords.

"I trust Saddam is well these days."

"Yes. Yes. Thank you very much, Henri," spoke General Tazmin jovially.

TWENTY-ONE

We were now in the center of the city and I could feel the dawn of civilization evolving underneath my feet. This was the valley of the Tigris-Euphrates. Where mankind, allegedly, first separated from the other monkeys and great apes. Mesopotamia this was. Civilization seemed to have stood still here as mankind flourished and branched out in all directions around the planet. A child grows up and moves out of his or her mother's and father's home. He or she then grows more, marries, and has and raises children of his or her own. And so on, and so on, *ad finitem.* Some children however, do not go on. They do not grow. They merely hang on. They stagnate. They may reproduce. But they do not grow. They do not further evolve.

I felt the darkness enveloping as we drove through the outskirts of Baghdad; then lift only slightly as we penetrated the more wealthy central part of the capital; towards Saddam's palace.

Our escorts pointed out sites of interest to us. Mostly to me as Henri was no newcomer to this city and society. The buildings were more beautiful in central Baghdad. More mysterious. More spiritual. Golden domes reflected the sun. Men in white robes and sheets covering their heads and bodies were to be seen all around. Women in long black robes, veils covering their faces walked several paces behind their men.

Saddam's face graced sides of buildings everywhere. No one seemed to be smiling. Except Saddam. The air hung heavy as we finally drove up to the palace and entered its grounds.

Armed troops turned the palace into a fort. We slowly pulled up in front of the main entrance and a foot soldier stiffly opened the limousine's door for us. His rifle was held at his left side, his right hand in salute as his commanders exited the black stretch Lincoln Continental after us.

Looking up at the Royal Palace between us and the sun, I wished I'd had another shot of that vile green liquid in the Lincoln. Lining both sides of the stairsteps up to the shiny metal doors were members of Hussein's elite guard regiment.

The foot soldier's four commanding officers turned around and perfunctorily returned their subordinate's salute. The foot soldier then slammed the car door shut, and the driver stepped out from behind the wheel to look up and salute his president and commanding officer as he emerged from behind the heavy gold-laden doors.

Saddam's smile had more of a chill in it than those of his pictured on his billboards and mosaics. It could be quite cold on the eighteenth green surrounded on all sides by a sand trap.

"Henri Beauchamps. My old friend. Do come in. I am sorry I could not greet you at my airport personally."

"Do not apologize so much, *Monsieur President*. It is not necessary." Henri belched. "Excuse me," he said as he delicately wiped his mouth with the back of his hand.

"Come in. Welcome." Saddam's expression did not change as he shook Henri's hand. "And—this is your friend?"

"*Oui*. Yes. This is my friend, Alain. He is to be my—uh—accountant."

"Allan? This accountant of yours—he does not have a last name?" Saddam looked me up and down. The gun on his hip grew like a third extremity from below the waist of the self-professed direct descendant of the Prophet, Mohammed.

"Allan Capstein," I heard myself nonchalantly reply.

"Allan Capstein?" He thought. "You are not related to *Paul* Capstein?"

"Paul is my older brother."

"Ah. Then. You *must* be our man." Saddam's smile was less friendly; more businesslike.

I felt myself getting excited. As if rising to a great challenge. Saddam led us up the stairsteps under the stone arch and through the heavy gold etched and sculpted doors.

Inside the walls of the palace, I was transformed back to Mesopotamia itself. Huge archways and pillars lined the halls and doorways while the center was clear beneath the encompassing dome. The floor came to life with ceramic mosaics of lions, birds, camels, etcetera under our feet. The marble walls had mosaics of plants and trees borne into them along with other exotic creatures of the savannah and forest. I easily could envision the huge orgies of food and sex that must have taken place underneath this great dome many times in the past.

"Allow my staff to show you to your quarters. You must be tired. You had a long flight. You must relax. We have plenty of time to talk."

Two more soldiers took our bags from us and led us up to a room on the second floor toward the rear of the palace. More portraits of the president adorned the walls leading to our chambers.

"You'd think he was the first and last leader this country's ever had," I told my buddy once we were alone.

"I told you he was not so bad. Didn't I?" retorted Henri as he threw off his shoes and lay back on his cot. He placed his hands behind his head and pulled his feet up close to his derriere under elevated knees.

"Are you for real? He gives me the creeps just looking at him."

"Relax. You're doing well. He's just another businessman, Alain. You just work out the details. The laundering. Leave the rest to me."

"You got it, *mon ami*. You got it."

I walked over to the dresser along the far wall and picked up an object that was sitting on its surface.

"Look at this. I wonder, if I rub it, a Genie'll pop out?"

"Try it, Capstein." Henri sounded almost as if he believed in Genies.

I rubbed the teapot and waited for results . . . Nothing . . . As I placed it back down a knock came upon our door. We looked at each other. A large fat man in a khaki uniform entered.

"Dinner will be served in half an hour. Would you be wishing for lamb or for beef? His black moustache twirled from side to side.

"I'll go for the lamb, please."

"Gimme *le boef*," replied Beauchamps looking up at our Genie.

"As you desire."

He bowed graciously and turned to leave.

"Do we get another wish, sergeant?" Henri was cleaning his nails with his pocketknife.

"How is that, sir?"

"That's only *two* wishes. Huh, Capstein?"

"That will be fine, sergeant," I replied. "Henri was trying to make a joke." I felt that cold hard knot of fear tearing through my gut again.

I had to admit it. Dinner was delicious. I almost expected Jean Tourneaux's cook and servant, Lucille to wheel out the babagonouch to us. Middle Eastern food was not new to me. I had often gone to some of the many Arab restaurants along Atlantic Avenue in Brooklyn for a good, inexpensive feast. Israeli food was almost identical to Arab food. I had been eating Israeli kosher falafel since I could remember. Henri had no difficulty at all making a pig of himself. Even in that dark pinstripe business suit of his, his manners came shining through.

Humis clung to his lips after he shovelled it up there with his pita bread. He used his napkin more or less as an afterthought after the backs of his palms did not do the job to his idea of perfection.

The liquor tonight was not green in color. The clear liquid was just as potent, however.

"You must relax tonight," declared our omnipotent host. Saddam stood at the head of the white linen-draped table with his glass raised in one hand, his other hand on his hip above his gun. The four trusted officers of his high command instantly raised their glasses in salute as Henri and I followed with our own glasses. "Business will wait until the morning. We will drink to our future. The future of Arabia. The future of our land!"

The President placed his glass to his mouth and drained its contents. We all followed suit.

"Tonight. There will be entertainment. For all!" He smiled toward his officers; then clapped his hands twice. "Bring in the music!"

The lights dimmed even more as two servants opened up a pair of double doors to our left. Presently, an eight piece orchestra marched in playing what I used to think was snake charming music while the two servants went behind them and set some oil lamps along the back wall ablaze. I soon saw I was right about the music.

A couple of minutes behind the orchestra came a lone clarinet-type instrument player playing a solo as he slowly entered followed by two beautiful, baubled, sheer veil-clad able bodied assistants carrying a large, weaved basket. The clarinetist sat down in front of the orchestra, crossing his feet and proceeded to charm a legless, scaly reptile out of its basket: the basket the two beautiful ladies delicately placed on the floor to his left side.

Once the reptile was out and climbing, one of the lovely barely clad ladies began her snake dance. The music pulsated. The thick diamond patterned black, straw and red reptile wound its body around its dancing partner's outstretched arm; then up her back and around her neck; then down her other arm. The snake's tongue flickered along its journey. The music swelled.

The Arabian belly dancer got down on her knees, holding her arms out in front of her, looking up at her pet, flickering her own glistening pink tongue back at him.

Then, the other beautiful Arabian belly dancer got down on her knees opposite her compatriot, and without stepping out of rhythm, offered one of her free arms to, at first, share the boa constrictor; then to dance away with him completely entwined around and through her body.

I barely noticed when Saddam rose up from the table to draw one of his generals aside. My heart was in my mouth. I absently drained my liquor glass dry, transfixed by the performance.

Then, to my utter shock and amazement, the belly dancer approached the oncoming general wrapped in her snake. The music grew in intensity. General Tazmin was nervous. Balls of sweat broke out onto his brow. What was making him do this?

I looked at Henri of all places in spite of myself. Henri subtly nodded toward each exit.

I turned and looked. The enlisted soldiers had their weapons drawn and pointed. Pointed at General Tazmin. The president stood out of the line of fire. His face had that same sinister smile reserved for his billboards and that humongous mosaic at the airport.

The general stopped and looked back over his shoulder at Saddam. The president looked at one of his troops to his side and flexed his head toward the general. The soldier moved in on Tazmin, a French made machine gun pointed at his commanding officer's stomach.

The general turned and resumed a reluctant approach to the nearing, twisting, snake-draped dancing lady. She held her arms out for the general. She placed her hands gently on his upper arms.

Tazmin stiffened. But he did not resist. That French produced machine gun was now digging into the back of his spine.

The boa constrictor slid calmly through her crotch, off her smoothly gyrating body, around her arm, and around and around the Iraqi high commander.

Tazmin did not move with the music with the same grace or smoothness as the Arabian belly dancer, as she moved away. He began to twist and squirm. The snake did not like that too much.

"You should not have been so greedy and ambitious, Oman. Only I in this room am a direct descendant of Mohammed. He would *never* let you take Iraq away from me."

"No! Saddam! You are mistak—" Tazmin's voice disappeared within the tightening coil of the constrictor. The music droned on as the two beautiful belly dancers kept up their gyrations on either side of him. The general was badly out of sync with the music.

"Do not worry, Tazmin. I told your wife you would be *late,* tonight."

A dull crunching sound could be heard just above the music as the coil collapsed to the ground. The clarinetist again broke into his solo as the two dancing girls moved back toward their reptile. Slowly, elegantly, the sparkling smooth boa constrictor slithered up and off the lifeless heap on the floor. Two of Saddam's elite guard moved in on cue from their divine leader and dragged the broken, red soaked body out the double side doors opposite the doors the orchestra first marched in through.

The two gorgeous belly dancers managed, keeping up their pulsating erotic rhythms, to very gingerly dance the now more relaxed cold-blooded animal back into its basket.

The entertainment, we were informed, was just beginning. Hussein told us the band was going to play us three or four *more* of his favorites.

"Do you have any requests, Mr. Capstein? What would *you* like to hear?"

"Whatever they want to play. Whatever you want would be fine for me, sir."

"Very well, then. Mr. Beauchamps. How about you?"

"Do they know anything by Mozart?"

"Mozart?" The president thought a few seconds. "How about the overture from *The Magic Flute?*"

TWENTY-TWO

I could not sleep at all that night. Every time I shut my eyes, I felt that boa constrictor around my throat. That cold hard knot in my stomach was now enveloping me. Even if I could get a few minute's sleep, Henri's incessant grunting and snoring would have put an end to it.

I knew now we had to get everything from Hussein in writing quickly, phoney as that gesture might be, before Paully could fly in here on Friday. We would have to take all our documents with us playing the charade to the hilt; then try to get out of this place alive.

Breakfast was served promptly at eight A.M. Henri came downstairs refreshed and unshaven. I was not hungry.

"Give me his portion," the pig commanded. *"La nourriture est tout grande, ici!"* Henri slobbered.

Coffee was good enough for me this morning.

"What is that next to your eggs?" I had to ask Henri.

"*Qu'est ce que c'est? C'est* lamb's organs. Spleen. Pancreas, *je pense.* Taste some." He held a forkful of some up towards me.

"No, thanks, Henri. They look like they might not be a spleen or pancreas at all."

"*Non? Alors—qu'est ce c'est?*"

"You think they came from a male or a female animal?"

Henri examined the contents on his fork more closely.

"Nah!" He looked some more. Then he put his fork down and wiped his face. With a napkin. "I'll have some more coffee," he yelled toward the kitchen.

Later that morning we were summoned to the Presidential conference room. I could think of nothing but the flight out of this desert the following day as we were escorted, by our friendly Genie, to the fateful meeting.

"Ah. Gentlemen. Have a seat. Make yourselves comfortable."

As Saddam waved his arm in our direction; then past us to our waiting seats, my back involuntarily stiffened. His arm appeared to be an exploding M-16 machine gun.

I placed my brown leather briefcase on the table in front of me and started to unfasten the locked hinges. Something grabbed my arms from the rear. Startled, I turned my head to see a pockmarked face with a chewed off moustache underneath a black military beret.

"That is not necessary, corporal. Mr. Capstein is to be trusted. He is the brother of the famous Mr. *Paul* Capstein." The corporal reluctantly let go of my arms. "Besides. I had his bags checked out last night.—While we were enjoying ourselves; getting to know one another better."

"Thank you, Mr. President. I hope you can trust us now."

"Sit down, Mr. Capstein. You too, Mr. Beauchamps. We two are *old* friends."

I thought I saw fear flash in Henri's eyes as we sat down. Why not? After all he *was* a human being, too.

"You are very thoughtful in your business dealings, Mr. Capstein. I know some of your clients."

"Is that so, Mr. President?"

"I made some inquiries. You are well thought of in your United States of America."

I continued to take some folders from my briefcase.

"Your Founding Fathers were visionaries in the New World." I looked up at him across the table as he spoke. "They knew thirteen colonies could not stand alone against one common imperialist enemy. They must unite to drive out the British. And stay united to *keep* the peace. And to prosper. Your greatest leader was Abraham Lincoln. He knew the Union must stay united if it were to prosper. Even if it meant an end to slavery. He knew the great potential of a *United* States. The untapped resources. The raw potential of the land. He was the *true visionary*. The *true strength and leader* of your land."

"Yes," I gestured. What else could I say or do for him?

"We Arabs are not unlike you Americans. We too have been colonized by the British. We made a great mistake though when we gained *our* independence. Instead of following your lead, we Arabs decided to set up monarchies. King of this State. King of that State. The same thing that has had you Europeans fighting and killing each other for centuries, Mr. Beauchamps. Too slowly you started to learn what the Americans figured out even before they left your continent to settle in the New World, I think. That is their strength. Their power today. Us Arabs? Today we must dissolve all these petty monarchies. End all this childishness.

"As your Abraham Lincoln has said, Mr. Capstein, 'We are all brothers. We must go forward together as brothers. Tap our natural resources as one . . .'

"Gentlemen. You are looking at the *true Abraham Lincoln* of all the States of Arabia. And in order to end our internal bickering—*our* civil war, if you will—I have solicited your aid. You have the missing part I need to shorten the strife. Shorten the needless suffering our people first under imperialist Britain felt, and now under these self-imposed Monarchs feel. I trust we understand each other."

"*N'est ce pas?*" shrugged my leery eyed friend from Marseilles.

"*N'est ce pas.*" I found myself agreeing. "No need to explain to us. This is *your* land. These are *your* brethren. I understand."

"You are a good man, Mr. Allan Capstein from New York. I think we can work out a beneficial agreement for *all* concerned."

Beneficial was some word for it. In exchange for all out nuclear war against his 'brethren', Saddam was willing to swap enough figs, dates and crude oil to keep our motors running and fig leaves in place for the next fifty years. Or, until the world melted away from too much of his thermonuclear pollution—or lack of enough ozone first.

Saddam Hussein could be quite ingratiating when he wanted to be. Havana cigars were handed out upon the filling out and signing, at my gentle insistence, of all pertinent treatises. Such as those specifying where and when certain Swiss establishments and institutions would be receiving Iraqi dinars and converting them into dollars and francs. Or, how certain public charities would be "buying" medical and/or health supplies from French suppliers Mr. Henri Beauchamps had close contacts with.

All in all, it was a deal any greedy pig without a human soul or conscience could live happily with.

Another green bottle of Schnapps was set on the table. The Abraham Lincoln of Arabia had five glasses poured out for us. One each for myself, Henri, the president's Minister of the Economy, Ochmed Abdullah on his right, his Minister of Defence, Surhan Al-Salome on his left, the last one for himself. Then, Abe of the Desert, in green fatigues, that revolver fastened to his hip and thick dyed black hair and moustache rose up, viscous glass in hand to propose a toast.

"To the future of the United States of Arabia. May we all march forward from here together. As Brethren. All tried and true!"

"Amen!"

"Praise Allah!"

"Yes. Praise Allah," the president echoed after consideration.

Henri drained his glass, wiped his mouth with his sleeve, gleamed. And belched.

"Amen," I saluted somehow.

Twenty-three

Delivery of the detonator was due the next day at approximately twelve, noon. That gave us the rest of this day and the following morning "to celebrate."

Saddam first took us on a tour of his milk factory. Right in the heart of Baghdad, across the street from an elementary school, it stood. The milk inside was all powder. But it was not white.

"Put on these face masks, gentlemen, when you go inside."

I looked at Henri upon examining the masks. They were gas masks. Beauchamps just shrugged it off and put his on.

"Without our detonator we would have to rely on this factory for our unification. Let us go down."

The president of his people, his *brethren*, brought us into the bowels of his chemical weapons plant.

"This is much cruder. Less precise. We ran a test of our latest batch on some of our own troublemakers last year. It does a good job. But only at closer range. For our purposes these substances have only limited uses. Our soldiers. They do not always like carrying them around in the field. They are like children, sometimes." Saddam paused with a patronly look on his puffy face. "Come. I will give you a demonstration."

"Great," exclaimed my friend, the pig from France. "I heard a lot about your 'milk' factory capabilities."

"Yes? From where, Mr. Beauchamps?"

"Oh," Henri mused. "You know Kleinschmeldt. The skinny German merchant. He told me about his tour along the northern border after the—uh—trouble there last year *dans les mountagnes.*"

"Hah. Yes. Heinz. A good friend. How is he doing these days? Do you keep in touch?"

After the small talk we were led into a dull metal room with black wire screens covering three or four circular openings ten to twelve inches in diameter along the base of the far wall.

"Check your masks, gentlemen." He watched us gleefully as we anxiously checked our gear for leaks along the edges of our faces. "Good.—Lieutenant Bazir.—*Release the specimens.*"

"Yes, sir!" came a reply echoing from a large speaker protruding from the top of the same far wall.

The screens slowly rose. Rats scampered into the center of our room darting past and under our feet.

"OK. Release the 'milk'!"

Suddenly, gas started leaking from the two adjacent walls to the door we entered from. As the dense cloud of powdered "milk" descended onto the rodents their squeaks and movement at first became frenzied; then spastic; then, nonexistent. All in the space of no more than fifteen to twenty seconds.

"Thank you, lieutenant."

"Yes, sir, General Hussein."

"We also have much slower working formulas. But for demonstration purposes, this is sufficient. Don't you think, my friends?"

"Very good, General," I exclaimed from behind my mask.

"Yes. But crude. It can be much harder to administer than you could imagine. With your help we will be saving time—and many more lives than you would think possible."

I felt as sick as those rats looked after about twelve or thirteen seconds into their "milk bath."

After Hussein completed the conduction of our grand tour of his pasteurization palace, he had us taken on a sight-seeing tour of his capital city. High up on the itinerary was the trip to the Grand Mosque. Today was not yet Friday. The Holy Sabbath in Islam. However, I was astounded by what we were about to see.

As we rolled up in our black stretch Lincoln Continental, we were witness to what probably would amount to the equivalent of a huge Catholic Mass. Only, this was Moslem. And, outdoors. In *front* of the Temple.

Hundreds of men, draped in white robes, all with covered heads and wooden headbands holding their white sheets in place, were kneeling. All in neat rows, evenly spaced. The High Priest, or whatever he must be called in this religion, was chanting—or singing—his praises to his God in front of his captive audience. Then, as one, they rocked forward and down, and kissed the earth beneath them.

The High Priest sang again. Then, suddenly, they rocked back on their knees and responded with a chorus of their own. Their musical strains echoed off the wall of the ancient Mosque.

"Why aren't they facing the Temple? They are all at a strange angle to the building."

Our guides laughed.

"Mecca."

"Mecca?"

"They are praying to Mecca."

"Oh."

Henri was not enjoying our trip very much. A frown was gracing his face as he kept looking at his watch every few minutes. Finally, he spoke.

"Perhaps you can stop off for a little while a *l'hotel* back there we just passed. They must have a pharmacy *dans l'entree.* A luxurious hotel as that."

"You are not well, Mr. Beauchamps?"

"It is just *mon estomac. Un peu* gas. Perhaps I could find *quelque chose* for it *la ba.*"

"Ah. Yes. But, we can return to the palace. Get something for you there."

"*Non. Non.* This is much closer. Much more convenient. *N'est ce pas?*—Oh!" Henri grabbed his stomach.

Our two armed sight-seeing guides looked at each other.

"I guess then," one of them answered, "it is OK with us. Driver. To the Hilton Hotel, please!"

We made a U-turn, leaving the congregation on its knees to take care of the business of Henri Beauchamps sudden stomach attack.

"*Alain. S'il vous plait.* Come *avec moi. Ton Angol,* it is much more good than mine."

"We will speak for you, Mr. Beauchamps. Why don't you stay here with our chauffeur? We will get you what is good for you."

"*Mais—*"

"Do not worry. We know the proper medicines for your stomach."

The less than benign smiles sent a chill up and down my spine. They left us sitting in a no parking zone, telling us not to worry. They would be right back.

As they disappeared into the Hilton, safely out of sight, Henri whispered to me. "Play along *avec moi.*"

"What?"

"Keep your voice low. Don't let this driver hear us. OW!" He grabbed his stomach and doubled up.

The driver nonchalantly glanced into his rearview mirror; then back out his window in the general direction of Mecca.

Looking up at me, Henri gestured for me to look at his inside coat pocket. He was holding it slightly exposed for me in his cramped position.

"What are you—"

"OH!" He closed his jacket again, grabbing my arm to shut me up.

"He all right?" The chauffeur glanced in the rearview mirror again and started to turn around. Henri clutched his stomach even tighter, protecting all the hidden documents he took from our business meeting earlier this morning with Hussein.

"He'll be fine. I saw him like this before."

"I don't want him throwing up back there. I have to clean it myself."

"Don't worry, driver. He'll be all right. Right, Henri?"

"*Oui.* Yes. I'll be—Oh—I need a little fresh air."

"Step out of the car, man. Step out of the car!"

The driver flicked the automatic door locks open, shot out of his seat and ran around the front of his limo to the right hand rear passenger door to assist Henri out into the street.

"What the hell are you up to?" I asked as soon as the driver popped out of the automobile.

"I have to find a fax machine in there!"

"Paully said to carry all the papers back with us. Then we can take care of everything when we get back on our own soil."

"*Oui.* And how about my pharmaceutical arrangements?"

"We can—We're gonna fax them with Paully."

"*Ah, oui?* I will fax them directly to my people myself!"

"Paul told us to bring everything to him, first."

"Do you always do as your older brother tells you, *petit frere?*"

"You're gonna screw us up here, Beauchamps," I pleaded.

"*Je ne pense pas, mon ami.*"

"Step out of the car, Mr. Beauchamps."

The driver opened the door that instant and pulled Henri by his elbow.

"I'm all right.—OH! I need a bathroom! OH!—"

"I have instructions, Monsieur Beauchamps."

"I do not care for your instructions. Can't you see I have to go?!"

Henri started hobbling to the front doors clutching his abdomen, flailing his free arm in the air back towards the driver.

"Do not make me do this, sir!"

I almost went in my pants as the chauffeur drew a revolver from a holster under the hem of his robe. He pointed it squarely at Henri's back.

The two tour guides came amiably back out of the hotel, down the three stairs leading from the main entrance at that point, just in time to appraise the situation.

"Do not shoot him, Abdullah!"

The chauffeur looked first to the two guides, then back to Henri racing up the three stairsteps. Slowly, Abdullah did as he was ordered and lowered his pistol.

"We have your medicine, Mr. Beauchamps. Here."

"*J'ai besoin d'aller le WC.* It is too late for that!" Henri looked at them earnestly and pushed the outstretched medicine away with his hand.

They looked at each other.

"As you desire. I will escort you inside," Saaid, the larger of the two men finally answered. "Tarrique will stay with Mr. Capstein and keep him entertained while I show you the way."

What class these guys had, I thought as the bulkier of the two escorts assisted the panicking Henri to the men's room.

Tarrique had some terse words in Arabic for the driver, Abdullah outside the limo. Abdullah, who had finally put his pistol back under his gown, tried to defend his actions. His arms flapped from his sides with his palms extending skyward toward Allah; his shoulders shrugged repeatedly up and down. Finally, Abdullah set himself back behind the wheel, shaking like a chilling vat of Jell-O.

"You do not care if I get out and relieve myself as well. Do you Tarrique?

"Well. I don't know." He thought a moment. "I do not see why not," he finally said after staring over the roof of the Lincoln. "Come. I will show you the way."

What a country. What hospitality. They did not even trust you to go to the bathroom and relieve yourself by yourself. They had to show you "the way."

Tarrique had a few more words for Abdullah. The driver stared straight ahead holding his wheel in both hands without answering. Then, Tarrique turned and gestured for me to follow him up the sun baked stairs and into the lobby.

Whereas the eloquence of this Baghdad Hilton rivaled that of Jean Tourneaux's hotel along the Promenade in Cannes, a bleakness prevailed even in here, beyond the darkness of the great sun drenched outdoors of Iraq.

I—we—found the men's room easily enough. Upon entering, I encountered Tarrique's partner, Saaid, straightening his headband waiting for Henri to finish up. Tarrique had enough trust in us to wait only just outside the front door.

"Saaid. You look beautiful," I sarcastically greeted him.

He glared at me, curling his upper lip, which caused his moustache to shift up along his cheek to cover his right nostril. Finally, having enough time to think, he spoke, his face dropping.

"You are making a joke."

"Yes. How did you know?"

"Mr. Beauchamps. How are you doing?"

The echoing belch of water cascading down the porcelain, gushing through the pipes answered his question for him.

"*Bien. Bien.* Much better."

Henri pushed the door to his private booth open and walked out, hitching his pants; then patting his stomach. I searched his eyes for any indication of what he might have done about his "pharmaceutical" papers.

"Alain," he jovially greeted me. "Take your time. Take your time." He grabbed me by my shoulders and spun me around; then looked me pleadingly in the eyes, his back to our overseer.

"OK, Beauchamps. We're in no rush." Saaid looked into the mirror at us suspiciously over his shoulder. "They got enough toilet paper here?"

"Look for yourself, *mon ami.*"

"Wait one second," interjected Saaid, his moustache again twisting up and over his right nostril. "I would like to make certain for you."

We waited and watched as the idiot entered the toilet booth and inspected it. He shook and rolled the remaining supply of paper. Then lifted and knelt over the toilet seat.

"Nothing wrong here, Mr. Capstein. You can use it."

"Thank you, Saaid. You are quite hospitable to us."

I entered as he held the door for me. Henri left the room without bothering to wash up. I caught Tarrique opening his arms in mock surprise and good will towards Henri upon his sudden reemergence from the lavatory before the door automatically resealed behind them.

Whatever Henri thought he was up to, I hoped and prayed it would not cause the cessation of my not-too-long life here on the toilet seat of this luxury Baghdad Hilton Hotel. How much more exotic could you get?

I thought of Marie back in Antibes as I sat there stalling for Henri's (and my) sake. And thought of Paul, too. I would have to prepare Mom and Dad for the shock of their lives: their older son's reincarnation after over a twenty year absence. Dad would not be as hard to prepare as Mom. He accepted Paul's "death" much better than Mom did. He became very stoic about the whole thing. When the war ended, and all the POW's came back that day on TV at Edward's Airforce Base in California, Dad turned and said, "Well. That's it. The boys are all finally back home," and went downstairs; back to his free pickles, hot dogs and other delicacies.

Mom sat there watching the TV. Staring; with eyes wide and raised eyebrows. I stayed there with her. When the last soldier came down the ramp and saluted and Paul was not one of them, Mom kept staring. The TV station broke for commercials. Yet Mom did not move a muscle. Thirty—forty seconds into the commercial break, she was still rigid. Transfixed to the picture tube. I asked her, "What's for supper," to try to pry her from the screen. "What? Oh . . . I don't know." She continued to stare at the screen. "We got hamburgers, Mom?"

"Hamburgers? What? Yes. Sure, Allan. Paully always liked hamburgers . . ."

"Mr. Capstein. You all right?"

"Yes. I'm—I'll be right out. Gimme a few seconds." How much more time could I stall in here? I took another minute, or so.

"Mr. Capstein. My camel cannot go for so long without more water. We cannot wait any longer."

I wanted to remind Saaid that we did not come here by camel this day. We took their stretch Lincoln

Continental. I hitched my pants up, flushed the toilet and slowly emerged, a bit more refreshed, physically.

"You are not used to the diet here, Mr. Capstein?"

"I guess not, Saaid." I shrugged my shoulders, tugging up my light grey wool blend pants about the sides of my too thick waist.

"Come. We must not keep the others waiting."

I could not figure how Henri could possibly reach a telephone—no less a fax machine—without our two good buddies, Tarrique and Saaid, watching everything, including our bathroom habits.

Out in the lobby, I saw Henri, of all people, in the glass enclosed gift and magazine shop. Browsing through a magazine. Would wonders never cease?

What a great idea, I thought. If I could only keep my concentration on a few English printed magazines between today and our anticipated exit from this "utopia" tomorrow around lunch time, I might be able to make it through all of this in one complete psychological piece.

I walked over to Beauchamps to see what he'd picked up off the shelf. I should have known.

"Marie still refuses to pose for them," he grunted over his shoulder.

Tarrique and Saaid were looking over his shoulders, as well, with great interest. Soon, the shop clerk walked over to us.

"Do you carry any American magazines?" I asked.

"American? Ah. Yes. Not too many. But a few." He twisted his head nervously for a second or two in the direction of the two Bobsy twins. They were too pre-occupied with Henri's "literature" to notice the clerk's look.—Much less return it. "Come. I will show you."

Around the other side of the stained oak magazine rack were American and British publications. I thanked him and began to browse through a copy of *Newsweek*. Donald Trump was on the cover looking de-pressed. Marla musta jilted him again, I thought. I opened it to my favorite page. The "overheard" col-umn and political cartoons. As I looked up for a mo-ment, I saw Tarrique and Saaid now holding for them-selves, and drooling over that same magazine Henri had been salivating over. I saw Henri nonchalantly take two or three steps backward and reach into his in-ner jacket pocket. Saaid busily turned the page and said something to Tarrique. The two of them turned to each other a second and laughed; then hurriedly glued their eyes back onto the pictures as Saaid slowly turned another page.

The English speaking store clerk just as noncha-lantly as Henri, walked back toward Beauchamps. I saw Henri turn away from the Iraqi escorts and slip his papers down from his inner jacket pocket to waist level. The very helpful store clerk brushed past Henri and glided over to our Iraqi tour guides, now ogling another Western girlie magazine from France.

The papers disappeared somewhere into the gift shop clerk's robes as Henri reached for another magazine from the rack in front of him with his other hand. I saw Henri whisper something in his ear as he brushed by.

The clerk's two countrymen looked up and around to him curiously as he passed Henri.

"I could put it in a brown paper bag for you gentlemen, if you would like."

Our two armed escorts continued to stare at the store clerk.

"No. No." Saaid finally spoke.

"Are you certain?"

"Maybe." Tarrique looked at his accomplice. "That would be all right with us."

Saaid looked back at Tarrique with fear in his eyes. Tarrique returned the gaze with a shrug and grimace of his own.

The hospitable Arab shop clerk took the sensitive Western document in question and wrapped it in coarse brown paper before slipping it into a thin, brown paper bag.

I fought back some laughter as the clerk demanded fifteen dinars for the contraband.

"Your stomach is better, as well? Ay, Alain?" Henri leered at me over the magazine in his hands.

"Much better," I retorted, looking at a cartoon of Saddam in *Newsweek* leading a band of warriors, sabres drawn, on camelback along the Kuwaiti border. The caption read, "We are only on maneuvers. We do not intend to invade our good neighbors to the south."

Our Iraqi travel guides were given their change and their package as I bought the *Newsweek,* a copy of *Time* and one or two other English language publications. We were then back on our way to finish our splendid tour of the nation's capital.

Henri did his business. And, we were still alive.

TWENTY-FOUR

It was amazing. How Henri could make a three hundred dollar plus business suit look like so many rags in just a day and a half. Yet, he did it. When we got back to our room in the Royal Palace, I asked him if he packed any other more formal attire.

"You mean like a tuxedo, *mon ami?*"

"No. I mean like another business suit."

"And what for? Our business is finished."

"Is it?"

"Your *frere* will fly in here tomorrow, give Saddam his merchandise and fly us away. *N'est ce pas?*"

I did not answer him.

"Cheer up, *petit frere*. We still have the night in front of us to kill."

"I'm not going *anywhere*. I bought these magazines to keep me occupied."

I picked the pile of them off the desk and tossed them onto my cot; then hopped up and lay down next to them.

"You do not want to insult our hosts, *mon ami*. Do you?"

"The hell with them. I just wanna get the hell outta this place. Death *lives* here."

"Ah. You are just not used to the ways of the Middle East."

"Life has no meaning to anyone here."

"You are exaggerating, Alain. They are just—how you say?—a little bit more down to earth here in some of their ways."

"You leave me speechless, Henri."

"*Bien!—Ici.* Look at *this* magazine *mon ami a l'hotel* gave *a moi* along with this business weekly."

He threw me a *LIFE* sized magazine called, *HOT DESERT NIGHTS.* A completely veiled Arabian woman was on the cover, kneeling beside a squatting two humped camel in the sand dunes. I opened the cover.

On the first page, still beside her camel, her face was unveiled. She was alluring. On page three, she was inside a huge tent with three other much more scantily draped Arabian ladies. The title of the following sequence of photographs was, LIFE INSIDE THE KING'S HAREM.

"Good stuff. Ay, Alain?"

"Not too shabby," I found myself admitting.

A few pages later, the leader of the King's Harem was back with her two humped camel. This time, totally unclad.

"You are a pervert, Beauchamps."

"I do not see you putting the magazine down, do I?"

"You are still a pervert!"

We both laughed. I'd actually grown to like and even appreciate this—this human being somewhat.

"Who was that guy in the hotel?" I asked.

Henri turned around on his cot and put his right index finger to his mouth.

"What guy? The clerk? Just because he put that magazine inside the business weekly? He also wrapped up that magazine inside that doggie package for Tarrique and his buddy. Did he not?"

"Yeah. You're right," I responded as Henri picked a pencil out of his pants pocket and scribbled something onto the inside cover of his French business journal. The look on his face as he handed the magazine to me told me what I should have suspected all along. The room was probably bugged.

I took the magazine from Henri and opened it up to page two. It read, "I met him there last year when I stayed at the Hilton. He knew how to provide his guests with some extra room service. *Comprendre?* He is good entrepreneur. A nice fellow."

A knock came on the door and I shut the *HOT DESERT NIGHTS* into the French Business Journal and stuck it under the mattress instinctively.

"You are requested for dinner, gentlemen." The fat Genie in military fatigues from yesterday reappeared with his insipid smile still under his moustache.

"Do we have a choice?" I asked.

"You still do not feel well, Mr. Capstein?"

"Well now. Now that you do mention it. But, it was Mr. Beauchamps who had the real problem this afternoon."

"Will you be joining us then, Mr. Beauchamps?"

"*Oui. Certainment.* I will be down. I feel much better now."

"Mr. Capstein?" The Genie's handlebar moustache added to the illusion of charm.

"Yeah. Sure. I'll be down. I loved the dinner last night."

"Good! The president wishes to *surprise* you tonight."

"Oh, boy." I looked at Henri. "We'll be down right away."

"Yes. Tell Saddam we are on our way."

"Splendid," remarked the sergeant. "You will not be disappointed."

"I am sure we won't."

Twenty-five

A few minutes later we had our shoes back on our feet. Henri tightened his creased tie and we started down to the banquet room. The fat sergeant was still on duty in front of our room when we exited on our way downstairs.

"These two lovely young ladies are the gift of our president, the Most Honorable Saddam Hussein for the evening." He bowed his head, opened his hands toward two young Asian women and smiled regally.

"Ah. You are much better looking than Tarrique and Saaid," gushed Henri nodding his approval at the Genie, then at me; then back at the girls.

Both young girls grabbed us by our arms, letting our imaginations run wild as they led us down the hall and on our journey to the banquet arena.

"Welcome. Welcome, gentlemen," greeted our gracious host upon our arrival. "I understand you did not fare too well this afternoon, Henri. I am certain these two young creatures will help ease any indigestion you may have experienced."

"*Oui. Oui, mon bon ami.* Your Vietnamese women really know how to cure a man's soul."

"I had the feeling you might already have known that fact, *mon bon ami.* Mei Lu and Rui-Wen will be serving you two tonight. Your every wish will be their command."

"This is most generous of you Mr. President."

"Please, Allan Capstein. You may call me Saddam."

"Thank you, Saddam."

"Girls. Show the gentlemen to their seats. The girls will fill your plates for you."

Saddam pulled out all the stops for us on this dinner. A smorgasbord was set up for us featuring all the delicacies of the Middle East.

"I'll have a shish-ke-bob, please," I asked the man behind the table in kitchen clothes and a chef's hat. Mei Lu, my escort took the sword from him in her right hand and presented it to me.

"Thank you, sweetheart."

"You are most welcome, Allan Capstein."

She bowed her head at me and smiled. This was going to be some enchanted evening. Mei Lu next took two pita breads and placed them on a plate for me.

"You will want something to drink, Allan?"

"Uh, yes. Yes I would." I looked at her. The yellow, orange and red scarves draping her supple body made her look like a ripe fruit waiting to be plucked from off the tree branch.

"I will pour you some red wine."

The meal was, of course, delicious. The dessert, divine. I forgot what I was doing there in Iraq after the second or third glass of Beaujolais. Mei Lu was an excellent hostess. She definitely knew how to take a man's mind off more worldly worries.

"I will not be insulted if you and Mei Lu wanted to go off somewhere for the rest of the evening, Allan. You deserve a relaxing, restful night tonight."

"Thank you, Saddam," I obliged.

"I can introduce you to her sister if you desire. Kui-Wai is at least as beautiful and fulfilling as her older sister."

I looked at Mei Lu a few seconds.

"It would be acceptable to me, Allan. I would not mind it."

I thought it over as she held my arm in both her hands, looking at me.

"No, Mei Lu. You are lovely enough for me this evening."

I don't know why I refused. It was always my most coveted fantasy to have two beautiful, willing girls at the same time. Some imperceptible sensation told me, not this time.

"You are sure, Allan?" spoke a startled Hussein.

I felt Mei Lu squeeze my arm a little harder. She had a strange longing look in her eyes.

"Maybe next time, Saddam."

"Suit yourself, Allan. Mei Lu will take you to where you can have more privacy this evening. Won't you?"

"Yes, General." She bowed her head to his icy stare.

"Have fun, Alain," leered a drunk French freelance arms merchant. "I will take her sister, if you do not mind!"

"I will send for her, Henri!"

TWENTY-SIX

Mei Lu led me to a secluded room all the way through and around in the back and down a winding marble flight of stairs. It was a long walk. But, this was no ordinary room. This sanctuary was designed for a Sultan's pleasure. Even better than the King's harem's tent, I thought. Its walls and ceiling were totally mirrored creating a mesmerizing effect. Everywhere I looked I could see Mei Lu and myself. In the center of this sanctuary lay a large canopied bed. I barely had time to wonder why the ceiling was mirrored if a canopy covered the king sized mattress. My young transplanted Vietnamese hostess immediately began to unbutton my shirt and loosen my neck tie.

I half-drunkenly grabbed her about her waist and pulled her closer to me. I smelled her beauty and kissed her neck. Then, I pulled away from her a bit.

"I will rub you with oil." She had my shirt off my back and my belt buckle coming undone. "Lie down on the water bed."

"Water bed, huh?"

"Lie down."

I did as she said. She went over to a dresser along the far wall and picked up a dark vase with a long neck and round fat bottom. She looked at me watching her in the mirror and came back to me slowly, dropping the veils from her shoulders, exposing herself to me from the waist up. Her tiny dark breasts were exquisite with those large black nipples pointing straight out at me.

She sat down on the mattress beside my buttocks, sending wave upon wave pulsating back and forth beneath me. She poured some oil into her hands.

"You should take your pants off, Allan. You will be much more comfortable that way." She started working the oil into my shoulders and down the backs of my arms.

"You don't have to do this, Mei Lu." I tried to raise myself up.

"You do not like me?"

"No. No. Yes. Yes. I do like you. You are beautiful, Mei Lu."

"Then. Why do you not want me to—"

"You do not have to do this if you don't want to."

"You *don't* like me!"

"Yes. I do like you. You are a sweet, beautiful girl."

"I do not understand."

"Why are you here, Mei Lu?"

"What?"

"How did you come to this country?"

The Oriental courtesan turned away. She looked down.

"Why do you ask?"

"How did you get here?"

"I came with my parents three years ago." I kept listening. "The government sent us."

"I thought so. Where are your parents today?"

"I am told they are in Tikrit. That is a smaller city north and west of here. They are working on a farm. At least, that is what they tell me."

I picked the veils up about her waist and placed them back over her shoulders. She glanced nervously back at me; then away again. "I have failed you."

"You have not failed me, Mei Lu. I almost—I almost—Why are you crying?"

"They will not like this. They will punish me for this."

"No. No they won't. You can stay here with me all night."

The young lady turned and looked into my eyes. "You are not like the others. The others just wanted to have sex with me."

"I can see why. Mei Lu—you are a beautiful woman."

"Thank you, sir."

"You can still call me Allan."

"Thank you."

"Will they ever let you free?"

"They say they will. In three more years."

"Then what?"

"If I could only get to Paris."

"Will they let your parents go too?"

"They say so. I do not trust them very much."

I started to put my arms about her shoulders, then hesitated halfway there, jerking my arms suddenly back. She looked up and laughed.

"You are a good man, Allan. I cannot believe you are an arms dealer."

"I can't believe it either."

"I will still give you a rubdown, Allan."

This time there was a twinkle in her eyes instead of sadness or fear. I looked her up and down.

"Do you have a girlfriend?" she asked as I hesitated.

"Um. Sort of."

"She would understand under these circumstances, I would think," she smiled. The bed began to rise up and down again as Mei Lu shifted herself more fully around, allowing her veils about her shoulders to slip again lower and lower and start to finish undoing my pants. "Would she not?"

"I guess so," I replied helping her unwrap the rest of her veils from the rest of her succulent body.

TWENTY-SEVEN

The next morning I awoke to find my clothes neatly piled and folded on a chair beside the mattress. I looked up through the oval opening in the top of the canopy to see only myself on the king sized mattress. I quickly looked around to see a thousand reflections of Mei Lu coming into focus, slowly revealing her body in the mirrors.

"What are you doing?"

"What do you think I am doing, silly?" she smiled, wrapping the thin multicolored material around her succulent breasts and flat belly. "I must get back to the kitchen. Who do you think does most of the cooking around this palace?"

"Will I see you again?"

"Thank you, Allan, for a most enjoyable and memorable night. I will not ever forget last night."

"Good luck," I grumbled as she enigmatically smiled, blew me a kiss and pulled the door shut behind her.

I slowly put yesterday's clothes back on myself and decided to go back to my room for a fresh shower and change of attire.

"Ali Baba," our fat Genie greeted me by the door, much to my chagrin, and took it upon himself, not unexpectedly, to usher me upstairs.

"I trust you had a good time last night, Mr. Capstein. Mei Lu has never disappointed any distinguished guest yet."

"I hate to leave Baghdad so soon, after last night," I played along.

"You will come again, I trust."

"Sure. Why not?"

We were soon upstairs at my door.

"I will wait outside, Mr. Capstein—while you straighten yourself together, as you say."

"I do?" He was almost amusing me. "You mean straighten yourself *up*. Don't you?"

"As you say."

I shut the door in his face. Thank God Henri was still snoring soundly. The room smelled from stale alcohol and perfume. He must be anesthetized, I thought.

Quickly, I showered, wanting to be out of this desert as soon as I could. Four more hours of this schizophrenia was more than I could take. While in the shower stall, I wondered how Paully was planning to take care of this Abe Lincoln of the Sahara. Maybe I *could* wait the four hours until noon.

I came out of the bathroom only to see my counterpart begrudgingly start coming back to life.

"Alain.—Oh!—*Ma tete!*"

"Morning."

"How was *your* last night?" He sat up, holding his head.

"Pretty good, actually. How about yours?" I dried myself off and threw the towel across my cot.

"My night?—Oh!—" Henri's head curved into his chest. "I do not remember."

"By the scent in this room, you musta had a great time."

"Ah. *Oui?*" He tried to straighten himself up, but couldn't make it.

"Trust me."

"*Je trouve.* I do, *mon ami.* I do."

I finished dressing and decided to pack up all of my things. The faster an exit the better.

"Try to get yourself together. You still got your bag to pack. Don't forget."

"Forget what?"

"Get yourself together. We gotta get the hell outta this place today. Remember?"

"Qu'est ce que c'est la grosse hate—the big rush—*mon ami?"*

I just looked at him pathetically scratching his skull—probably looking for lice—and tied my shoe-laces.

Breakfast came and went slowly. It held little taste for me, even though I knew who must have prepared it. How could she ever endure another three years with these people? Prostituting herself for these mad-men. Maybe there *was* some merit for us being in Vietnam twenty some odd years ago. What kind of a government can justify trading its people to other countries in order to pay off its debts? This was simply unbelievable to me. I could not even begin to wonder how Paul felt about all of this.

I left over half my toast and scrambled eggs sitting on my plate and excused myself.

Soon, we would be going to Saddam International Airport. And out of here. I wished I could have smuggled Mei Lu and perhaps her younger sister out of this hell hole with us. I was sure Henri Beauchamps would not have minded that too much.

At exactly eleven-fifteen on my wristwatch, Ali Baba came knocking on our door.

"Gentlemen. The president, *mon General* is waiting for you."

I looked at Henri. He was paler than I had ever noticed him to be before.

"C'mon, Henri. Grab your bags. Let's get going."

"*Oui. Oui.*" He sat up painfully.

"I will assist you, Mr. Beauchamps. That Rui-Wen and the other one. They really know how to wash a man out. *N'est ce pas?*"

"*Wear* a man out, Sergeant."

"Yes. *Wear* a man out. *N'est ce pas?*"

I thought I would be the one to puke first. My eye caught the teapot we thought Ali Baba first came out of on the dresser when I bent down to lift up my suitcase.

"Do you believe in Genies, Sergeant?"

"Genies?—Oh.—You mean like that American TV program with the astronaut. I have an entire flock of them, Mr. Capstein. We call them *wives* here in this part of the world."

I looked at that insipid smile under his black handlebar moustache and tried to keep my half-eaten breakfast down instead of decorating his uniform with it. Somehow, it worked.

"C'mon, Henri," I called. "The fresh air will do you some good."

"*Oui, mon ami. Oui.*" He lumbered along raggedly behind me.

Saddam's black stretch limo was waiting for us. Ali Baba opened the door for us; then he threw our luggage in the trunk.

"Come in, my good friends. Come in. Your brother is flying in himself to deliver the merchandise. Paul Capstein. He is a man of his word. That is why I could trust you from the outset, Mr. Capstein."

Saddam's smile betrayed the fact he already told me how thoroughly he checked me out beforehand. Or how he had my briefcase searched while we were "enjoying" ourselves over dinner with him and his two—or three—snake charmers.

"Thank you, Saddam. You are a most hospitable person."

"I trust you enjoyed yourselves last night."

"Yes. I did have a pleasant night."

"You are most modest, my good friend." The creep slapped and grabbed my knee. "Mei Lu is my personal favorite. You should have gone for her sister as well."

"Yeah," I managed.

"And you, Henri. How can a man of your stature and reputation have such a big hangover as this I see?" Saddam looked at him, amused.

"Do not speak so loudly. *S'il vous plaît.*"

Everybody laughed. Except Henri. Saddam's three remaining, highly trusted officers were in tow with us to the airport. Saddam opened the bar.

"Anybody besides Mr. Beauchamps want a glass?"

"*Non. Non,*" moaned Henri amidst the laughter.

"I'll take a drink," I declared. I needed one.

Paully's words rang in my ears. *"Just play it straight. Go through all the motions and play along with everything. You'll be fine."*

"Drinks for everybody! Henri Beauchamps will drive his hangover away with this." Saddam reached for a freshly poured glass of that viscous green liquid and handed it to him.

"Merci," I heard him reply.

"To Allan Capstein and Henri Beauchamps. Two good friends of Iraq."

"Amen."

"Praise Allah!"

"Salut!"

"Amen!"

Finally. Past the clumps of saluting foot soldiers and tank masters along the main highway. And, smiling, "benign," towering portraits of our gracious host, we came to his airport.

"I trust we will see each other in the future soon again, gentlemen," bade Lincoln of Arabia.

"Yes," I retorted, raising my almost empty glass in his direction. That cold, hard knot in my stomach had long since worn thin and frayed through. I figured I had become immune to all this international intrigue. Just then the sound of a lone jet propelled aircraft came straining over the bright, unblemished western horizon.

"Another drink, my friend?" the president asked.

"Yes. A short one," I insisted, staring westward over the plains.

"We will meet him on the runway," asserted Hussein.

"Good." I let him pour some more Schnapps into my glass.

"To the future," I saluted.

Hussein nodded as did his right hand men.

"To runway number two!" Saddam ordered his chauffeur. I could not help noticing that Abdullah was still his chauffeur today. I was not sure he'd even still be alive at this point, considering the sharp words and tension from Saaid in front of the Hilton the day earlier. Things did, indeed work in mysterious ways in this country.

The gem of an airplane glistened in the sun as it descended from the heavens. The sooner aboard the better.

The lustrous jewel grew larger and larger as it approached the earth below. Finally, it touched down on the stretched out asphalt in front of us. The roar grew in intensity as the sparkling diamond raced toward us.

We were all standing on either side of the black limousine as Paully rolled up and approached us. Only I anticipated danger, I thought, as I alone knew Paully's *true* mission.

"Just like your brother. Not one minute late. How he survived behind enemy lines in the jungle has never been a mystery to me."

Saddam looked very pleased. *Why not?* He was soon to have the means of achieving total control over all the oil and gas fields of the Middle East; with the possible exception of those oil and gas fields he promised to me and Henri Beauchamps yesterday morning. If he did not die for it first.

Paul saluted with a thumbs up from the cockpit as he pulled up to our right on the runway.

"Who is that next to him?" Saddam turned to his three remaining most trusted henchmen.

"Looks like—Yes—It is Viktor Durzinsky. What is *he* doing here?" asked Colonel El-Mali.

"Who do you think was able to come up with the actual merchandise, gentlemen?" I thought quickly. "Viktor still has his contacts in the Russian military. Some a their top military scientists are hungry. They see the handwriting on the walls of the Kremlin. They will soon be unemployed too over there in Moscow."

"Yes. What a fool, this Gorbechev. He is disassembling his own power all over the world! Soon, everybody will be looking *this way* for spiritual guidance." The self-proclaimed direct descendent of the Prophet Mohammed patted his stomach and arched his chin ever higher.

The cockpit of the French fighter plane Paul and Viktor flew in on began to hiss open. It brought back General Tazmin's dancing partner, the boa constrictor, to me for some reason. I felt this entire nation was wrapped up in a boa constrictor, choking whatever life it had left in it out of everything and everyone.

"Ah! Greetings, Paul Capstein." Saddam approached my brother with a large smile and open arms.

"Greetings, my good friend. Greetings!" They embraced each other warmly.

"And, I see my old friend, Viktor Durzinsky is with you."

"Yes."

"Greetings, Comrade Hussein. So good to see you after so long a time."

"Yes, Comrade Durzinsky. But, you were still with KGB back then."

"Times have changed, Saddam."

"Yes. Times have changed, indeed." The dictator squinted his eyes at Durzinsky. "I see you are now working with Mr. Capstein."

"I go with the times. One cannot live in the past. It is not good for your health, Comrade Saddam." Viktor nodded and looked into the eyes of Saddam Hussein and his three commanding officers. "I do not see General Tazmin today. Is he taken ill?"

"You might say that, Viktor Durzinsky."

"I see."

"Yes. But enough of this small talk. Where is my merchandise, gentlemen?"

The madman was smiling. His three henchmen stood flanking either side of him as if prepared to draw their weapons.

"Where are our agreement papers?" Paul's smile was all business.

"Paul Capstein. I am surprised at you. You seem distrustful."

"Not at all, Saddam. Perhaps we could exchange items on board the airplane." Paul's smile grew in determination.

"Yes. But your brother, Allan already possesses all your originals."

Paul looked at me. I nodded.

"They're all in my briefcase, Paul," I lied.

"Great. Then. We can get things all concluded right now. Where's your briefcase, Allan?"

"In the car."

"Great. Go in and get it and we can—"

"Colonel Yahwinh will get it for you. Go, Zahir."

"Come to the plane, Saddam. Everybody. We can examine everything together."

I lost feeling in my body as I mechanically began to follow everybody, once Colonel Yahwinh reemerged from the back section of the black stretch Lincoln, and handed me my briefcase. That schmuck, Beauchamps took all the damn papers he needed to launder himself through his phoney pharmaceutical company and gave them away! I *knew* he would screw things up for us sooner or later.

I kept following everyone with a plastic smile on my face, mostly for Zahir's benefit as he walked beside me.

"Hello, Allan." A strangely familiar voice yelled out to me from inside the body of the jet fighter.

"Who is this here?" insisted the Lincoln of the Sahara.

"This is my flight assistant, Guy Du Berge, General," obliged my brother, Paully.

"Guy *Du Berge?*" mused the maniac. "Another relative? You are not related to—"

"Michelle Du Berge. He was *mon pere.*"

"Guy?" I was shocked to see him sitting there. Never mind that his Canadian skiing trip must have ended quite abruptly. His voice *was* familiar enough for me. Nothing else save for his lanky relaxed body language looked the same.

"My ski trip was finished. *Alors.* I came back to France."

"You look good. You managed a great tan in the mountains."

His hair also turned color. From wavy black to straight blonde. Gone too was his bushy moustache.

"*Oui. Merci.* The skiing was great!"

I could see he was leaning on a brown wrapped package the exact same color and size as that five pound package he handed to me, obviously in disguise, at the airport in New York City. Was *he* going to be the hit man? Who here was more innocent looking?

"Sit down, everyone. There is enough room. Is everything in order, Allan?" asked my brother.

"Let me give it a final going over for your benefit, Paul."

We all took a seat; except for General Ohmir and Colonel Yahwinh. They stood just inside the cabin, guarding either side of the hatchway, facing everybody.

I took the papers out carefully, and soberly thumbed through them.

"They are all there. *N'est ce pas?*" demanded the unshaven French wino, Beauchamps shakily.

"Looks good, so far, Henri," I answered busting his chops a bit.

I looked up and about the cabin. The Iraqis were all staring at me. Saddam was sitting back; still with a benevolence about him. He obviously trusted me enough to not pay much attention as to whether all the documents were actually in my hands or not. His bald-headed Lieutenant Colonel, who seemed to be filling General Tazmin's niche, sat next to His Highness just as contentedly as his leader. I gambled that the other two men were either too far away or, as usual, too paranoid; preoccupied with anticipating any other irregularities on our parts to be concentrating on whether or not I did have all the papers with me. What did they care? They already knew they didn't steal back any of the agreement papers from us.

"So, Allan. Everything Kosher?"

"Yeah, Paul. Perfect."

I went into a brief description of all we were supposed to get out of the "deal" and how I was going to be able to keep things hidden and "Kosher" for everyone concerned.

"Good," Paul confirmed. "Guy. *Le paquet?*" Paul nodded at the object Guy was still leaning on and smiled in the direction of Saddam and his officers.

"Here you go, man!" He lifted it up to his chest like a basketball. The two henchmen bent their elbows, raising their open palms to their hips.

Guy seemed not to notice. Total innocence marked his face. He stood up from a squat and held out the package for the Lincoln of Arabia to accept.

"Thank you, young man. But, Viktor. My old friend. You may have the honors."

Saddam raised his right arm and opened his palm in Durzinsky's direction, asking him to unwrap what I had unknowingly been brainwashed into carrying across the Atlantic—so that I might be reunited with my long lost older brother.

"As you wish, Comrade."

Gingerly, Viktor took hold of the box and un-wrapped Saddam's belated Christmas present. There it was. Black as the limo outside on the runway. Shiny new. Five color coded wires extended from its base.

"It is simple, my friend. You insert the device on the top of your weapon just below the war head. Then: follow the visible light spectrum as the key to where to place each wire. Look here." Viktor hooked eyes with those of the evil dictator. "Make certain this rod here firmly locks—*securely*—into the reactor compart-ment. Otherwise . . . Hmm?" Viktor nodded his head and shrugged. "You will be reunited with your Mohammed sooner than you expected."

"Let me see."

The fearless leader took his gift from the former KGB agent and examined it closely.

"You probably will need to refine the shape of your cases in order to secure the perfect lock."

"That should not take too long. A few weeks. A month at the latest. We can manufacture more of these now, too." He kept drooling over his belated Christ-mas present. "We can hold off any outside interference at least that long."

"So. We are all finished here then," Paully con-cluded.

"Yes, Mr. Capstein. It has always been pleasant dealing with you. Next time—we will roll out the red carpet for you in the United States of Arabia, my brethren!"

"You got it, Mr. President." My brother got up and embraced the maniac again.

"Guy. The champagne!"

"Yes, sir!"

Guy turned around and reached behind him. The two Iraqi henchmen stiffened again in anticipation.

"Ici, Monsieur Capstein." He held up a bottle of Dom Perignom for all to see.

"Amen!" Henri finally stuck his two cents into the goings on.

When was the hit coming? How were we to get out of there alive afterward? Even if they *did manage* to hit the three men on board this aircraft here along with Hussein—there was still Abdullah, the chauffeur to reckon with.

We all toasted our alliance. Only Paul abstained. He was to fly us out. *That was it! He would do the hit himself!* I drained my glass quickly, hardly tasting its elegance.

"I apologize to you for having to leave so soon. But, we must be goin'. The Deputy Premiere expects me for dinner in Paris at six o'clock. I have to cover my tracks."

"Yes. You do, Mr. Capstein. It has been a pleasure, Allan Capstein. Henri. We will meet again, soon."

"Thank you so much for last night."

"For you. Anytime. You too, Henri."

They finally got off the plane, brought us our suitcases and got into their stretch Lincoln. I thought they would *never* leave us.

"Guy. Secure the cabin."

"Yes, sir, *Monsieur* Capstein!"

"I thought you were gonna take care of him," I said to my brother once Guy pulled the hatch shut, blocking the insane party from sight and sound.

"Stop worrying, Allan. Strap yourself in so we can take off."

"But—You're letting him get away!"

"Oh yeah?"

What was I missing? I saw that twinkle in Paully's eyes.

"Guy?"

"Yes, sir."

"Not until our wheels are off the ground, son."

"Yes, sir!"

"Allan. Look outside the window for their car when we're airborne. You won't wanna miss it."

"Oh yeah?"

We started to taxi down the runway.

"Wave to them, gentlemen . . . That's the way. Bye, bye, *mon Fuhrer.*"

The jet engines raced faster and faster. The asphalt and sparse shrubbery sped by. The nose of the plane tilted skyward. The rumble of rubber on asphalt ceased.

"Now, son."

"Yes, sir!"

Guy reached behind him to where he had pulled out the bottle of Dom Perignom. He pulled out a smaller, yet matching shiny black box to Hussein's prized detonator and pressed a bright red button on its top.

"Five minutes and counting, sir."

"Well done, Guy."

"Good boy," added Viktor Durzinsky from the copilot's seat.

"*Merci, Monsieur Capstein. Merci, Monsieur Durzinsky.*"

"How was your stay in—"

"You son-of-a-bitches! You used me. I could have been killed if they suspected!"

"They always suspect, Henri. They are worse even than KGB or CIA could be."

Victor and my brother, Paully looked at each other.

"Fuck you, Durzinsky. You are causing me to lose millions! Billions of Francs!"

"Dinars, Beauchamps. Dinars. They are Iraqi. Not French."

"Fuck you, Capstein. This will ruin my reputation."

"Hah! We are salvaging some of it for you, Comrade. Your father could even be proud of you now for this."

"And how about my dummy charities back home?"

"Yeah. I told ya he'd try to figure a way to fax them something, Viktor. Didn't I? Tell him what happened there, Guy."

"Are you sure, sir?"

"Go ahead. Leave out the mechanics."

"Well. I took care of the telephone system for them. We got your faxes at *Monsieur* Tourneaux's—ah—*Monsieur* Tourneaux received the faxed papers. No one else."

"*You* were the one who bugged my computers."

"Oui. That one was fun. I love to do computer graphics."

"You are good, kid." I shook his hand.

"*Merci, Monsieur Capstein.*"

"Time to buzz over the highway. We don't wanna miss it!"

"Keep up your altitude. You do not want to dip into their range of fire."

"Yes, sir!" Paully sarcastically smiled at Viktor.

Paully arced his aircraft back to the east. Once again Baghdad approached us below.

"Time, Guy."

"Four oh eight, sir."

"Fifty-two more seconds."

Fifty two more seconds. Then, bye-bye, Saddam Lincoln of the Desert. Fifty-two and counting . . .

"There's the road, boys. Thirty seconds in fronna us."

"Four twenty-five . . ."

"There. There they are!"

Twisting down the two lane highway back to his palace rolled their black stretch Lincoln Continental. Rolling just past one of his smiling toothy larger-than-life billboards.

"Four thirty-five . . ."

"Keep your altitude, Capstein."

"Funny, Viktor!" The two ex-adversaries turned to look each other in the eyes a split-second; then back down the road underneath and in front of them.

"They are pulling off the road, Paully!"

"Shit!"

"Four forty-five . . ."

"Look at the Son-of-a-Bitch. He's goin' up behind a bush."

"What a pisser!" Paully had not lost his sense of humor even now. "He's still within range of the limo. Got 'im with his pants down, huh?"

"Ten . . . nine . . . eight . . ."

"He sees us. He's looking up at us. *Shit.* Look at 'im running away with his dick in his hand!"

"Four . . . three . . . two . . ."

Three doors to the Lincoln simultaneously tore open and four bodies sprang out from different directions like jack-in-the-boxes, looking up at us, and started to—

"*One . . . BLAST OFF!*"

The four jack-in-the-box puppets were instantly swallowed up in an exploding inferno. A fifth body further from the inferno went flying in the same trajectory it was running in seconds earlier. That fifth body came to rest, face down, motionless in the sand.

"Let's get outta here, gentlemen. They still have war planes that can intercept us before the border."

"Think we got him, Paully?"

"We'll know soon enough, Allan. We're on our way home."

I prayed he meant the United States. *Of America.* Not just France.

"Watch the screen, Vik."

"No need to worry. We already have an all clear to come and go."

"Use your head, Comrade. The all clear to go would never be granted before the exchange was completed."

"Use *your* head, Comrade Paul. We made good on our exchange. They bought the package."

"*Oui. Et Saddam. Il est morte. Pour certainment. N'est ce pas?*"

Henri just made me airsick.

"Watch the screen, Vik."

"How far to the border?" I asked.

"Twenty-two minutes. We'll make it back home in no time."

I held my breath for the next what felt like a day-and-a-half.

"I heard Mom broke her hip last fall. Huh, Allan?"

"You knew about that?"

"I know she's gettin' around without her walker these days."

"I'll break the news to them, Paully."

"What news?"

"C'mon. Be serious."

"I am serious. There were no guaranties made to me here."

"We *got* him. What more could the president want?"

Paul did not answer.

"We did get him, Paully. No Iraqi fighter jet tried to intercept us. What more could the guy want from you?"

"*Ah hah. Alors.* You sold me out for your president? *Je comprendre maintenant.*"

"Shut up and sleep things off, Beauchamps. You still are a disgrace to your family."

"You owe me one for this, Capstein."

"I'll remember you at Christmas."

"*Oui.*" He grabbed the unfinished bottle of Dom Perignom and brought it to his mouth.

Only Henri Beauchamps would have enough couth to drink Dom Perignom straight; without using an intermediary object such as a glass of some kind. Let alone a wine goblet.

TWENTY-EIGHT

"*Allo.* Welcome back, Alain!"
Marie ran up to me and hugged me tightly as we stepped out of Paully's yellow BMW. I hugged her back just as tightly and would not let go.

"I missed you, Alain."

"I missed you, too."

"You do not look well."

"I—I am great. I'm fine." I was perhaps feeling a bit guilty over poor Mei Lu.

"*Ici.* Come in. I know what you could use." She grabbed my arm and led me into her kitchen. "Come inside, everybody!"

"Have some iced tea *avec* lemon, Alain."

She poured me a large glassful not awaiting an answer.

"*Ici.*"

I drained half of it on the spot.

"Ahhh . . ."

"Voila!"

"Voila." I tried to let the nightmare within me subside.

"Personne d'autre? Iced tea?" She held up the pitcher for all to see. "How did it go?"

"I'll take a glass, Marie," spoke *mon frere.*

"I'll bring it to you, Paul," spoke Poon Li breaking away from him.

"Merci. Non," begged Viktor.

"Oui, Marie," answered her brother.

A certain uneasiness began to permeate the house as she poured some into a large tumbler for her brother.

Henri snapped on the TV set and tuned it to CNN. Everybody that flew that mission gathered around the set. Marie and Poon Li looked at each other, quickly sensing that our mission may not have been a success.

Marie came over and sat down beside me on her yellow sofa as Poon Li remained in the kitchen.

Finally, something started to come out.

"Unconfirmed reports are coming out of Iraq of an attempted coup in Baghdad this afternoon . . . We will keep you posted on any further reports or developments . . ."

"What happened?" Marie finally asked.

"Guy blew up his limo. But, he decided to step out and go to the *W.C.* first," I responded.

"Oh, *non.*"

"You *ruined* me, *Monsieur* Capstein. My partners won't want to do business with me anymore after this!"

"Your partners will forgive you, Beauchamps. Give 'em some time to think things over. They'll soon realize you were set up. *You* would never put nuclear destruction ahead of profits!"

"The phone is ringing, Marie."

"*Oui.*" She rose to answer it.

"*Oui ... Oui ... Monsieur* Capstein. It is *Monsieur* Tourneaux." She held out the receiver to Paully.

"*Merci, mon cherie.* He extended his left arm to take the call.

"*Oui? ... Oui ...* He does? ... Why didn't you tell him to call me here? ... Hah, hah, hah. This phone is safe ... *Alors* ... Wait a minute! They are talking again on TV about it ..."

"*We now have more details on that coup attempt in Iraq. It seems that three of Saddam Hussein's top officers were killed while attempting to take Saddam prisoner somewhere outside of the capital city of Baghdad. Saddam's personal chauffeur and body guard may also have been killed while attempting to protect the Iraqi President. Hussein himself is reported to have sustained a broken leg and dislocated elbow in the fracas that took place along the main highway that runs from Baghdad to Saddam International Airport. We will keep you up to date on this story as it unfolds ..."*

"Jean . . . Looks like we missed the target . . . Just broke one of his pegs and maybe an arm . . . Yeah . . . Yeah . . . Maybe . . . Maybe . . . *Merci*, Jean . . . *Merci*."

I looked at Paully. His smile was not so mischievous as he looked back at me.

"Cheer up, Allan. It ain't the end of the world. The president called Jean's place looking for me. He heard the first report on CNN, too. At least, he knows we tried."

"I'm gonna stay a few more days here in France with you, Paully."

"No. You are going back to New York. You have a business firm to run back there. I'll get home some time."

"What should I tell Dad?" I hung my head down crushed with the stupidity of that question.

"Tell him you had a great time on the beach here. Look at that suntan you got there, kid."

I unconsciously examined my arms and the backs of my hands.

"It's hot in the desert."

"It's even hotter in hell."

"Oh, yeah?"

"That's what they tell me."

"Poon Li." She was now standing in the living room, drying her hands on a kitchen towel halfway between the telephone and the TV set. "Any time you are in the States. She can come. Can't she?"

"Yes. I can, Allan. And, yes. I will arrange to visit with you."

"Good. Good."

"Stop all this gloom. We now know how to keep in touch. My people will talk to ya, Allan. We'll see each other again. Besides. The president.—Hah. Charlie got to be President. What's this world comin' to?—Charlie's a strange guy. Once this recession you got goin' over there ends, and the elections are over with, there's no telling what he might say. He's gonna call me tonight over at Tourneaux's place. Jean just told me."

"What happened to that meeting with the Deputy Premiere in Paris at six o'clock?"

"*What meeting* with any Deputy Premiere in Paris at six o'clock?" Paul's sly smile started to light up his face again, lifting my spirits. "That was just an excuse to get the hell outta there without having to stop off an stay for a free lunch. Come to Cannes tonight. We'll do up the casinos and night clubs before you leave for Fun City tomorrow."

"The Big Apple."

"Yes. The Big Apple. I forgot they changed Gotham's name again in all these years."

Twenty-nine

"Hello . . . Hi, Charlie. Long time, no see."

"You missed the creep."

"Shoulda seen him running with his pecker in his hand. Think we blew it offa him."

"We're gonna step up our efforts in the United Nations if he invades Kuwait."

"Expect it any time now, Chucker."

"We on speakerphone? What's that echo?"

"I got someone wantsa speak to ya, Charlie."

"Who's that?"

My brother edged me to the phone. He pointed his palm to the mike; then swept it at me.

I looked at Paully; then back to the telephone.

"Hello, Mr. President. This is Allan Capstein. Paul's brother."

"Oh, yes? So . . . How's your accounting firm doing these days?"

I looked at Paully, my eyes wide. Paully just smiled calmly back at me.

"All right. I guess."

"I hear you think we're in trouble these days with the economy."

"Well. Now that you mention it. We're predicting this recession will last a year-and-a-half longer. Detroit is hemorrhaging. They may have to scale back to stay afloat."

"Yes. We've been watching that here. We're gonna try to entice Japan to buy more of our goods in the future."

"You might do well to think about placing more tariffs on *their* goods, Mr. President."

"That's a tough one. They probably would not like that. We need ta keep them on our side."

"We need to keep our people working, Mr. President."

"We're on *your side,* Mr. Capstein. Things are not as bad as you are implying. Don't believe the press so much, Allan."

"Yeah." I looked at Paully with disbelief. Was this a moron I was talking to? Unemployment was now at its highest since the last great depression. And rising steadfastly. Paully half-smiled back, gave me a wink and a nod of his head in confirmation of my findings. How *did* this guy get to be President?

"I see Paul saw fit to get in touch with you, Allan."

"Why can't he come back to the United States, Mr. President?" Bile rose to my throat, making it harder to breathe straight.

"Your brother should not have involved you in anything, Allan. He was running illegal drugs in Vietnam, you know."

"Yeah. And from what I can figure out you were in on it too."

"Did your brother tell you that?"

"No. He did not. But I can—"

"Hey. I didn't even take over the Agency till *after* the war. What'dya tell him, Capstein?"

"Enough. Without mentioning any names."

"Well. We're gonna hafta keep an extra good watch on you then, Allan. When you get back to the States. We don't want any decent people back here getting unnecessarily hurt. Do we?"

"We both just put our lives on the line for you. Along with some other people. Don't you think my brother deserves a break already? What happened in Vietnam was close to twenty years ago!"

"Your brother was always an idealogue. Always with his highfalutin sense a right an wrong. We made a deal here. He did not deliver."

"You are full of bullshit, Mr. President."

"Hey. I like you, Capstein. You don't fool around. Paul. You there? Your brother's a tough cookie."

"He always was, Charlie. He always was."

"Better tell him ta wise up. He's got a business here ta care about."

"Don't worry, Charlie. I didn't trust him with any names or dates. He won't say anything anyway."

There followed a tense silence on the other end of the line.

Then: "Paul. I wish I could let you back. You are even more of a patriot than I am in a lotta ways. We got an election comin up next year. I can't risk anything right now."

"I understand. How's Betsy?"

"She's fine. Thanks. You still with that Oriental lady?"

"Yeah. She's right here."

"Hello, Mr. President," Poon Li said with an edge of sarcasm.

"Hello, there. Maybe we all can meet next year after November if things work out."

"Is that a promise?" I asked.

"My campaign promise to y'all. How's that sound to ya, Paul?"

"Good as gold, Chucker. Good as gold."

"And you, Allan. Don't you worry about the economy, Allan. I would not call it any kind a recession yet."

"I know."

"Yes. Well. You just play your cards right, now. And maybe we'll all see each other in Washington in the not-too-distant future."

"That would be good," I responded.

"Great. Well. I hafta be goin' now. Nice talkin' to y'all. Bye."

"He's a prick." I turned to my brother when he hung up.

"He's not so bad, Allan. He's a politician. You have to understand that. If he doesn't get reelected—some other prick will."

We all erupted in laughter.

"You think he meant it? He's gonna let you back in?"

"I don't know. He sounds sincere enough this time. Half the guys involved in the drug operation already went down in the Iran-Contra thing anyway. It shouldn't be able to hurt him too much if he wins re-election anymore. He'd stay clean enough from it."

"He likes you enough to let you back?"

"He *owes* me enough. C'mon. Marie and Tourneaux are waiting for us in the casino. Let's go down there."

"Paully?"

"What is it kid?"

"Never mind."

"Never mind what?"

"Nah. I just was picturing you that day you went off to the airport with Dad."

"I'll be back after the elections, Allan."

"Yeh." I managed a smile, cleared my throat; then embraced Paully before walking toward the elevators.

"So. You're still taking Marie to the Big Gotham."

"Yeah. Sure. Why not?"

"You looked a little shaky when you first saw her this afternoon."

"It was a tough flight over."

"Oh, yeah?"

"I slept with a young Vietnamese girl there last night."

"I gathered something like that musta happened."

"Oh yeah?"

Paul did not answer right away.

"They have 'em practically like slaves over there, Paul." Again, Paully did not reply. "What a lousy planet we're living on."

"It ain't so bad, Allan. The creeps hafta be kept in check. That's all."

"Yeah."

"So. You still like Marie after last night?"

I looked first at Paully; then at his girlfriend, Poon Li.

"Yeah. I still like Marie after last night."

"Good. She still is stuck on you."

"We'll drop you two a postcard, then."

"Great, kid. C'mon. Let's hit the casino. I wanna shoot some dice tonight."

We walked off the elevator and across the lobby to the gambling arena. Tourneaux and Marie were waiting for us at the slot machines.

I went over to Marie and hugged her from the rear. She turned around and kissed me back on my cheek.

"Je gagne deux centaines et cinquante—I won two hundred and fifty francs. Alain! *Ici!"* She reached down and held up a bag for me to see. She was radiant. I was blissful. I spent the rest of the night thinking how things were going to be back in the Big Apple with Mlle. Marie Du Berge the next couple of weeks. At least. That, and trying not to think of how on earth I would be able to bring myself to be able to work for the reelection of that fine upstanding President Shrubman of ours—in order to bring Paully back home to us again next fall.

Leonard Leventon